THE NIFFITS

DONALD F. AVERILL

INK START MEDIA
5710 W Gate City Blvd Ste K #284
Greensboro, NC 27407

Chapter 1

Strange Happening

Twelve-year-old Roxanne Maxwell was in her upstairs bedroom, windows wide open, listening to music and working at the detective station in her closet. Her current interest was solving neighborhood crimes. Someone had thrown a rock against the Maxwells' garage and she was dusting it for fingerprints. She had collected most of the neighbors' prints from their garbage cans. Out of the twenty-seven neighbors, she was only missing three sets of prints from the elderly. It had been a painstaking job; she had no assistants. Her closest friend, Dexie Chappell only seemed to want to read.

"Hey, Roxy! How'd you like to go to the store?" Five-foot nine Carl Maxwell called to his daughter from the driveway. Mrs. Maxwell, Mary, had given Carl a grocery list and suggested he take their daughter, Roxy, with him to the supermarket. Roxy knew more about the brands her mother usually purchased than Carl did. Carl's attitude about food was, if Mary cooked it, it was going to be good. He didn't drink but had developed a paunch that had forced him to punch another hole in his belt. There was only room for one more hole or buy a bigger belt. A bigger belt was not an option. His bald spot had grown larger in the last year from scratching his head at work.

Carl worked for the city as an electrical engineer for a suburb of Portland, Oregon. When on the job, he was very observant, but when relaxing at home his mind oscillated erratically between home and work. He occasionally solved job problems at home, sitting in front of the TV but not really watching, his mind mulling over snags at work. Mary noticed her husband's mind was somewhere else once in a while, but usually, the most severe lack of attention occurred when she wanted him to help with housework, although he didn't mind mowing the lawn or taking care of mechanical and electrical problems. He disliked doing laundry and washing windows, but vacuuming wasn't so bad.

Mary had given Carl a wink when she asked him to make a trip to the store for her. Combined with the grin and a twinkle in her eyes, Carl knew the wink meant a special dessert. A vision of strawberry shortcake smothered with whipped cream crossed his mind, but he didn't want to buy a bigger belt. He quickly got up from watching TV. Carl folded Mary's list and poked it in his plaid shirt pocket. Actually, the wink from Mary hadn't been necessary for him to get out of his chair. He couldn't remain sitting for any length of time. Having his body in motion was natural; he wasn't going to have a heart attack from being out of shape. He actually enjoyed mowing the lawn with an old push-type reel mower. Sometimes he got annoyed with all the motor-powered lawn equipment. One of the most annoying machines was a leaf blower that some of his neighbors used—too often.

Saturday afternoon was Carl's usual time for doing home maintenance projects, but only after a football game in the fall. Roxy enjoyed helping her dad. Father-daughter time had been less this last

year than was normal; his crew was short-handed so he had to put in extra hours. Roxy possessed an uncommon interest in tools and wanted to know how everything worked. Carl didn't have a son, but it rarely crossed his mind, he couldn't imagine having more love for a child, boy or girl. He thought it was great to have two loves in his life. When they went places, he enjoyed walking between the two women. They were almost the same height, too; both were five-six brunettes, Mary just a fraction of an inch taller than Roxy.

Mary would have gone to the store but there was a cake in the oven and she didn't trust anyone but herself to remove the angel food creation at the correct time. But in order to get dinner prepared the way she wanted; she would have to send hubby to the supermarket assisted by his able sidekick.

"Okay Dad, I'll be right there." Roxy had leaned toward the window and called out. Roxanne C. Maxwell was very bright, so smart she sometimes amazed her parents with her knowledge, and they were both college graduates. The *C* in her name was for Catherine.

Roxy's current art interest was making collages from dried flowers. She had picked flowers from the entire neighborhood in her quest to find just what she wanted to construct a collage of Mt. Hood during the summertime. Mt. Hood was a beautiful sight even though nearly forty miles away. The glaciers at high elevations gradually shrunk under the summer sun but winter snows made them stand out vividly against the blue sky. It was Saturday before school would begin, right after Labor Day, the first Monday of September. She was looking forward to the seventh grade, new teachers, her own locker, and new friends.

Roxy put away her glue, grabbed her purse, and on the way through the kitchen, swiped her right index finger around the inside of a bowl her mom had used for the cake mix. The door slammed behind her as she ran out to the car licking the batter off her finger and wiping her wet digit on her nearly worn-out jeans.

She rolled her eyes back in her head and said, "Umm. I can hardly wait for the cake."

"Hey smarty pants, what's in the cake?" her dad queried.

"Banana flavoring, sugar, and vanilla, for sure," Roxy replied, pleased with her ability to distinguish influences on her taste buds. "Flour and I think some eggs, too. Roxy skipped around to the other side of the car and waited for her dad to press the unlock button on the ignition key. Carl reached into his pocket and withdrew a ring full of keys. Several coins fell out, bounced on the concrete, and went into the grass.

"Nuts!"

"What's wrong, Dad?"

"Oh, I dropped some change on the ground and it went into the lawn. You can get the coins when we get back. That'll be your pay for coming with me," Carl grinned.

Carl pressed the unlock button and the door locks clicked open. Roxy opened her door, jumped in, fastened the seat belt, and sat waiting as her dad slid into the driver's seat.

"I hope there's at least one quarter in the change you dropped. I think I deserve a raise in my allowance—a middle school adjustment." She grinned and looked straight ahead through the windshield.

"Might have been. I didn't see the coins, just heard the noises. Sounded like three or four coins hit the pavement, mostly pennies I think."

"Jeez Dad, how am I going to get rich from you?" Her impish grin was not unusual when with her dad.

"Not from me, dear. You'll have to work hard and get good grades. Maybe you can go to medical school and support your mom and me in our old age." Carl chuckled.

"Hey! That sounds like a good idea. I'll be able to experiment on you and Mom with some new drugs." They both laughed.

The trip to the supermarket took about thirty minutes, but they were gone for nearly an hour. Roxy wanted to get some new jeans so they stopped at a mall clothing store where she dashed in, tried on one pair of pants and used her dad's credit card. Carl didn't mind her occasional use of the card because Roxy understood the word thrifty. He told her it was part of her birthday, which was coming up in about nine months.

When she got back in the car with her purchase, she leaned over and gave her dad a peck on the cheek and said, "Thanks, Dad."

"You're welcome—I needed that."

As they were coasting back up the driveway, Roxy released her seat belt and rose up from her seat to see if she could see any coins in the grass. She was too far away from where Carl had dropped the coins, so she sat back down and waited for the car to come to a stop.

By the time her dad had released his seat belt and opened the car door, Roxy was already looking through the grass for the coins. Carl picked up the grocery bag, slid out of the seat and stood beside the car door watching his daughter scan the grass.

"Look Roxy, over there," Carl pointed with his left index finger.

Roxy looked about four feet to the right at the bottom of the three steps to the kitchen and saw four coins in a neat row on the concrete. Two pennies, a dime and a quarter were lined up on the cement next to the grass. She squatted down and picked up the coins, dropped them in her pocket and said, "I thought the coins were in the grass, Dad."

"You'd better ask your mom about that, Roxy. She must have taken a break from baking and found the money I dropped. I'll bet she heard me say 'nuts' when we were getting in the car. She probably heard me mention you could have those coins, too. She must have lined them up so you couldn't miss seeing them."

Roxy entered the kitchen, took a deep breath of the wonderful scent of a baked cake and asked, "Mom, did you find the coins in the grass and put them next to the first step out by the driveway?"

"I don't know what you're talking about, dear. I've been in the kitchen ever since you left with your dad. Oh! I take that back. I did take out some garbage about thirty minutes ago, but I didn't see any coins by the steps. Sorry."

"Well, I'm going to fingerprint the coins and find out who did it."

"All right dear," her mom answered, not paying much attention to what Roxy said. Mary was amazed how many things Roxy did. Not yet a teenager, Roxy was busy with new projects all the time, never running out of things to investigate.

Carl began to unpack the groceries from the plastic bags but Mary gave him a hip and shooed him away. Carl turned to leave the kitchen, thought better of it, turned back around, put his hands on his wife's waist and kissed her cheek and then her neck.

"You're slowing down my preparation of dinner, dear," Mary smiled.

Roxy had run up to her bedroom, picked up a playing card, rushed back down to the coins, slid the card under the coins and took them back to her crime station. She avoided touching the coins with anything that would disturb the prints and slid the money off the card onto a sheet of shiny paper, which she placed in the top compartment of her five-drawer evidence and hobby box.

The second drawer in her cabinet held a little container of powdered cocoa, a small soft bristle paintbrush, which Roxy also used for watercolors, and a dispenser of transparent tape. She opened the third drawer, which contained her stamp collecting paraphernalia. A watermark tray and fluid, stamp hinges, magnifying lens, and stamp tongs were neatly stored in drawer number three. The only other thing she could get in that space was a few loose stamps ready to be mounted in her worldwide album.

Roxy picked up the stamp tongs and grasped the quarter from the evidence drawer with the long-nose tweezers. After placing the coin on a new sheet of paper, she opened the cocoa and gently sprinkled the light brown powder over Washington's head until there was a thin layer covering our first president's features. Roxy wondered if the first president had ever had a cup of hot chocolate. She closed the container of cocoa, picked up the paintbrush and just using the tips of the soft bristles, gently brushed off the loose powder.

Roxy had been holding her breath as she performed the delicate operation and was suddenly gasping for air. She turned her head to the side and took a deep breath, but when she inhaled she felt a sneeze coming. Not wanting to contaminate her sample, she jumped up and turned away from her hobby desk and sneezed. She wondered if the neighbors heard it, the sneeze was really loud. Roxy grabbed a tissue and blew her nose. She opened the tissue and could see some tiny brown spots, telltale evidence that she had inhaled some of the cocoa dust.

Resuming her position at the desk, Roxy took a piece of transparent tape and gently applied it to the surface of the quarter. She lifted the tape and affixed it to a clean piece of paper and wrote down the details of the fingerprint. But, when she looked closely at the tape, there was no evidence of a print; just a few tiny specks of cocoa powder had been lifted from the surface of the coin.

After fifteen minutes Roxy had eight pieces of tape attached to her paper with annotations about each sample. There was one problem; no fingerprints were found on any of the pieces of tape. The coins had been wiped clean!

Chapter 2

The Trap

As Roxy put her investigation tools away, she began to consider what animal, besides a human being, might have put the coins by the step. Several creatures came to mind, a raccoon, a rat, a bird, or a squirrel, or perhaps a monkey. She didn't think any monkeys were loose in the neighborhood, someone would have told her mom about it. The neighborhood housewives were a pretty gabby group, especially the elderly ones. So why would an animal put the coins in a straight line? And why wouldn't the culprit take the shiny objects back to its nest or burrow? Roxy thought, "I've got to go online and find out which animals might do something like this."

The young detective spent over an hour investigating animals that steal. Roxy couldn't find anything about an animal that would find coins and align them where the money could be easily seen, but she found videos showing animals taking things to eat or hide. Roxy checked her watch. Dinner was less than an hour away. She planned to ask her mom and dad if they had any ideas.

As they were eating dinner, there was a lull in the conversation. Roxanne was pondering how to ask about the coins. She didn't have to think very long.

"Roxy. Did you figure out how the coins got there all lined up?" her dad quizzed.

"Nope, but I've been working on it. None of the coins had fingerprints on them, so I suspect a small animal did it."

Roxy named the animals she had been considering and mentioned her Internet search hadn't given her any further clues.

"Could it have been another animal, a little bigger?" her mom suggested.

Roxy frowned, looked at her mom and said, "For example?"

"Well, two come to mind, Dean and Dexie."

"Did you see either one today, Mom?" Roxy asked.

"No, but you know me. When I'm working in the kitchen, I'm oblivious to things going on around me. One of them might have come to the kitchen door."

"But they would have knocked, wouldn't they? Besides, I think Dean would have kept the money. Dexie would have taken the coins and given them to me at school."

"I guess you're right about that. What do you think, Carl?"

"I'm thinking I have to mow the lawn tomorrow," Carl replied.

"Dad! You're not helping me."

"Yes I am, Rox. I gave you thirty-seven cents and a new pair of jeans today," he grinned. "Okay, I have an idea. I'll help you build a trap and we'll see if we can catch the money finder/organizer. How about that?"

"Oh, thank you. That would be awesome. When can we start?"

Carl didn't answer immediately. He was chewing some of his dinner. He swallowed, took a sip of ice water and said, "The earliest we can start on it would be after I have a piece of that cake your mom baked combined with a cup of coffee. Say, what about some ice cream, too?"

Roxy laughed. "I thought you were going to say next weekend. That would have been excruciating! Oh, Dad! What about your waistline?"

"My, such a big word!" observed her mom.

Carl smiled and said, "I think I'll start on a diet tomorrow." He smiled, "I thought Roxy was going to say that would have been really crappy."

"Carl! Your daughter doesn't need to be exposed to your workers' vocabulary."

"That's okay, Mom, I've heard much worse than that from my friends. Some of them say things using foul language I don't even understand."

"And your friends talk like that? Maybe you need some new friends?"

"Not Dexie, Mom," she smiled, "She's nice almost all the time. I've never heard her say any bad words."

As soon as dessert was finished, Roxy and her dad got a pad and pencil and sat down at the dining room table. They began designing a trap to catch the animal exhibiting the strange behavior, while Mrs. Maxwell started the dishes.

"I've got some wire screen out the garage, but how big should we make it, Rox?" asked her dad.

"If it's a good-sized bird like a crow or a magpie, the trap needs to be at least the size of a shoebox," Roxy replied. "If the animal is bigger than that, we'll have to make the trap bigger."

"Okay. If it's a raccoon, the trap will have to be much bigger and stronger," her dad commented. "We'll try the shoebox-sized first and see what we get—if anything. Let me draw a diagram of what I'm thinking about. Then we'll talk it over and adjust. Okay?"

Carl started drawing and Roxy watched as the trap took shape on the pad. Roxy watched as squiggles and straight lines appeared from the tip of the pencil, fascinated by the electronic circuit symbols her dad drew on the back of the paper. Someday, she would understand how to design and make electronic circuits.

"Okay, Roxy. Here is what we're going to make. We'll take a penny and clip on two tiny wires so the coin will be part of a circuit. If an animal disturbs the circuit and pulls one, or both of the wires free, the latch holding the cage open will release and the opening will snap shut, capturing the culprit."

"Oh! That sounds good, Dad. Is it battery powered?"

"Yep! We'll use a nine-volt battery and put it and the circuit in a little plastic box outside the cage with two wires to the coin and another two conductors to the latch. We should be able to construct it tomorrow and have it ready for testing on Monday."

"Awesome! You can show me how to solder, too."

"Okay. I'll have to get a smaller, low wattage soldering iron for the electronics. The one we have is for household use and is too powerful for integrated circuits, it will get too hot and ruin them. Tomorrow, we'll visit Radio Shack. We might have to get a few other things, too. But, right now, I need another piece of cake!"

Before Roxy went to bed, she had an idea. She took a penny, stepped outside the kitchen door and dropped the coin in the grass near the position her dad had dropped the coins earlier in the day. She thought, "Will the penny be on the concrete next to the bottom step in the morning?"

Roxanne had a difficult time getting to sleep that night, thinking about the coin she had dropped in the grass. "What if the penny is still where I dropped it in the morning? But, if it is, whom or whatever moved the first coins might not move a coin in the dark. Maybe they only do things during the day, but would they risk being seen? Hmm."

Chapter 3

Assembly and Testing

Sunday began as a sunny but lazy morning. Roxy woke up about seven o'clock, pulled the covers around her neck and stretched her legs. Her bare feet struck the cool sheets at the bottom of her bed. She was suddenly wide-awake, jumped out of bed, pulled on her slippers and ran downstairs to the kitchen.

She couldn't get out the door fast enough to see if the coin had been moved. Her pajama leg caught on the lowest part of the screen door, pulling her pajama bottoms down about six inches. She looked around to see if any neighbors were watching and pulled her pajamas back up to cover her exposed buns. The screen door, released from her clothing, slammed shut.

"Roxy! Is that you?" quizzed her mom.

"Yes, Mom. Sorry I woke you."

Roxy stepped down to the concrete driveway and looked at the bottom of the steps.

Nothing! Disappointment was the wrong word to describe her feelings; devastation was a more appropriate description of how she felt. She scanned the area of the lawn by the steps and could see the penny standing on edge supported by several blades of grass. Frustrated, Roxy went back in the house, locked the door and went back to bed.

She pulled the covers over her head and thought, "I'll tell Dad we don't need to make the trap."

"Roxy! Time to get up! Breakfast!" her mom tapped on Roxy's bedroom door.

The preteen turned down the covers, rotated her legs out of bed and sat up, yawned, and wiggled her toes. She put on her slippers, grabbed some clean clothes and headed for the shower. As she went in the bathroom and shut the door, Roxy could smell the scent of shaving cream her dad had used a few minutes earlier. She hadn't heard him in the upstairs bathroom.

After showering and getting into clean clothes, she dropped her pajamas and some underwear into the hamper and went down to the kitchen.

"Good morning Roxy."

"Morning, Mom and Dad."

Her mom replied, "Want some orange juice, dear?"

"Yes, please."

"Guess what, Roxy?" her dad quizzed.

"What, Dad?"

"Take a look below the bottom step outside."

Roxy jumped out of her chair, ran to the back door, flung it open and nearly ripped the screen door off its hinges. She stared at the bottom step but didn't see anything. Roxy stepped farther out on the landing and looked down at the driveway below the step. A coin! Was it the penny she had dropped in the grass the night before?

She picked up the one-cent piece and checked the date and mintmark to make sure it was the same penny. Roxy looked closely and read 2009 D. Lincoln had a scratch across his forehead. "It's the same penny!" She was sure of it. She grinned and opened the screen door.

With the penny in her fist, she went back to the breakfast table and sat down. Opening up her hand to show her parents the penny, she said, "Did one of you put the penny at the bottom of the step?"

Her mom answered first, "Not me, dear. I haven't gone outside this morning."

"Nope," her dad replied, not even glancing up from the Sunday paper.

"Then how did you know it was there, Dad?"

"I went out to the garage for the box of electronics parts this morning after I picked up the paper. When I came back in the house, I saw the penny. I left it right there so you could see it."

"But I checked for it earlier—at 7:00 a.m. and the penny was still in the grass."

"I guess the culprit wasn't up yet when you looked," Carl smiled. "Maybe whoever did it was taking it easy on Sunday morning? Maybe they went to Sunday school."

"Dad!" Roxy shook her head. "When can we start on the trap, Dad?"

"Eat your breakfast and I'll have another cup of coffee, then we'll get busy. Do you have an empty shoebox we can use as a template for the cage?"

Roxy was chewing a bite of waffle and couldn't answer immediately. Her dad waited for her to swallow. She swallowed and took a sip of orange juice.

"Yes, Dad. I've got a new pair of shoes in a box in the closet. We can use that shoe box."

"Make sure you take the shoes out, Roxy," Carl smiled.

Roxy ignored her dad's teasing. "Don't we have to go to Radio Shack?"

"Nope. I found everything we need in my junk box. I forgot I had a low-wattage soldering iron."

The morning was cool and there was still some dew on the grass when Roxy and her dad went to the garage to start fabricating the cage from metal window screen. Roxy had goosebumps, so she ran back in the house and donned a blue sweatshirt. She grabbed the shoebox from her closet, dumped the new shoes on her bed and returned to the garage.

Carl smiled and said, "I was just about to ask you where that shoebox was."

In about half-an-hour, the cage was fabricated. Roxy and her dad had only used three tools: tin snips, a hammer, and a pair of pliers. A metal rod was used as a pivot for the hinged side of the cage, which would be put on the ground and concealed with dirt and grass clippings. A spring was stretched and fastened so it would snap the door of the cage closed when a coin was pulled from one or both of the tiny clips holding the disk in the middle of the cage on top of a thin layer of dirt.

Carl had used a small solenoid to strike a rod holding the cage door open. When the circuit containing the coin was conducting, the cage would be open. As soon as the coin was pulled away from one of the clips, the device would react, knocking the rod away and the cage would snap shut. At least that was the theory.

Carl showed Roxy how to solder the necessary wires and attach the battery and the tiny clips to the coin. When they were ready to test their device, they heard Mary calling, "Hey you inventors, time for lunch."

"Okay, dear, we'll be right there."

Lunch was rather light, tuna fish sandwiches, celery sticks and a little peanut butter, and some fruit. Roxy ate a banana and had to wash her sticky fingers afterward. She was so excited about testing the cage, she ate too fast and got the hiccups. Her mom told her to drink some water, which she did. Adios to the hiccups.

As the family was finishing lunch, there was a knock on the front door.

"I'll get it!" Roxy slid from her chair and ran to the door in the living room. She turned the lock and opened the door.

"Hi Dex! Come in."

It was Dexie Chappell, her best friend from down the street. Dexie was about an inch shorter than Roxy and a little bit heavier, wore glasses and had shoulder-length reddish-brown hair. Dexie was an avid reader, digesting romance novels, sometimes as many as three a week, although during the school year the quantity slowed to about one per week. Homework took precedence. Dexie purchased most of her literary material at garage sales and some of it was very exciting. She had to share the thrilling parts with her buddy, Roxanne.

"What are you doing today, Rox, anything interesting?"

"Come up to my room and I'll tell you all about it. It's kind of strange, but exciting."

"Roxy, who was at the door?"

"Nobody, Mom," Roxy laughed as she looked at Dexie.

"Who is it you're talking to?"

"It's Dex, Mom. We're going upstairs for a bit."

They got comfortable on Roxy's bed and Roxy related the incidences with the coins. Dexie listened very closely as Rox related her story.

"So, you think it's an animal, like a bird or something?

"I don't know what it could be. Can you think of anything, Dex?"

"How about catching whatever it is?"

Roxy got excited that her BFF was on the same wavelength.

"Yes! Dad and I built a trap to do just that. It's in the garage. Come on, I'll show you."

Roxy grabbed Dexie's left hand and jerked her off the bed, almost pulling Dex on top of her. They stumbled to the hallway and started down the stairs, laughing at their clumsiness.

When the almost-sisters arrived in the kitchen, Dexie said, "Hi, Mr. and Mrs. Maxwell!"

Carl and Mary acknowledged Dexie's greeting and Mary said, "Where are you girls off to?"

Stopping momentarily, Roxy stated, "The garage. I've got to show Dex what Dad and I put together this morning."

The girls continued through the kitchen and out the door to the garage, the screen door banging behind them.

Carl yelled after them, "I'll be out in a minute. Wait for me!" Carl drained the last few drops from his coffee cup and started out to the garage. He looked at Mary, grinned, and said, "I think we've created a monster."

Mary smiled and replied, "Yes, dear, and we have to feed and clothe her until she's eighteen, and then there is college," she sighed.

Roxy was explaining the details of the trap when Carl joined the girls in the garage.

"Let's test it, Dad!" Roxy said excitedly.

"Okay, but let's have Dexie spring the trap 'cause she doesn't know what to expect."

Carl installed the battery and slid the switch to "On."

"Okay, Dexie, take the needle nose pliers and try to get the penny from inside the trap, but don't put your hand in there," Carl instructed.

Dexie picked up the pliers a little hesitantly, looked at Roxy and her dad and then at the penny. She carefully pinched the penny with the tips of the pliers and pulled on it. The trap suddenly snapped shut and knocked the pliers from her hand.

Dex jumped away from the trap. "Oh! Geez, that scared me!"

The pliers were in the trap with the penny and Roxy yelled, "It works! Now we can catch the magician that's playing tricks with the coins."

"That's very clever, Mr. Maxwell," complimented Dexie. "I wish my dad could do things like that."

"Thank you Dexie. I'm sure your dad has other talents. Say, what's your dad doing today?"

"Mom and Dad went golfing today at the country club. They left me home so I could do some schoolwork and some more reading. I'm reading a novel called *The Last Straw*. I finished the first chapter and thought I'd come visit with Rox for a while."

"We're glad you came over, Dexie. Thanks for testing Roxy's trap. Now that we know it works, you guys can set it up and see what you can catch. But you had better wait until I mow the lawn, something I promised I would do today. What is that novel about? It sounds interesting."

Dexie looked a little startled that Mr. Maxwell would be interested in what she was reading. "It's about a female secret agent helping a French policeman solve a crime in Paris."

Carl nodded and checked the oil level on the lawnmower's wheels and moved the old-fashioned mower to the front yard. When he was out of earshot, Dexie said, "I was a little surprised your dad was interested in my literary interests. My mom and dad never ask me what I'm reading."

"Where'd you get the book?" Roxy wondered if Dexie had gotten it from the library.

"There was a garage sale over on Pine Drive. I bought a sealed box of books for five dollars. I didn't know what was in the box," she shrugged. "It's an adult book, but so far it's pretty interesting."

Chapter 4

The Trap Stayed Open

The girls went to Roxy's bedroom and talked until they no longer heard the lawnmower slicing through the grass. It was nearly 1:30 p.m. when they retrieved the trap from the garage. They had run out of gossip and it was time to set up the metal cage to see what they could catch.

Carl was putting the mower away when the girls entered the garage to get the newly constructed animal trap. Roxy picked up the cage but forgot the small rod that held the shoebox-sized enclosure open. Carl noticed they had forgotten the little rod, picked it up and followed them to the driveway by the kitchen porch.

The girls were down on their hands and knees on the grass next to the steps to the kitchen door. Roxy had opened the cage door to insert a penny in the circuit when she realized the rod was missing.

"Do you need this?" Her dad grinned and held out the metal rod.

"Oh, thank you, Dad. What would I do without you?"

"You would have used a stick or gone back to get the metal rod in the garage. You girls are pretty resourceful."

"Thanks, Mr. Maxwell," Dexie smiled. "You'd make a good teacher."

Dex and Rox propped open the trap and put some dirt and loose grass over the bottom of the trap on the ground and inserted the penny. The girls noticed the trap was not very heavy and they were afraid it might get knocked over by a reckless human's big foot.

"What happens if the trap gets bumped, Dad?"

"I know how to fix that. Get four of the big gray nails from the bench in the garage. They're in a small cardboard box below the hammers."

Roxy was gone for about fifteen seconds, returned and dropped to her knees. She held four large gray nails in her hand.

Carl looked at Dexie and said, "Do you know why the nails are rough and gray, Dexie?"

"Is this a quiz, Mr. Maxwell?"

"Well, —kind of," Carl smiled.

"No. Why are they rough and gray?"

"The nails are coated with zinc so they won't rust."

"Oh. So, they cost more. I'd just use the cheap ones," Dexie stated and smiled.

Carl gave up attempting to make the experience educational. He had the girls poke the nails through the trap door into the ground, one nail on each corner of the cage floor. Roxy tried to tip the cage over but it hardly budged.

"Thanks, Dad. That was a good idea."

"You're welcome." Carl stood back and looked at the trap. "It looks like you're all set. Let me know if you need any help, okay? I'm going in the living room to finish reading the Sunday paper."

"Okay."

Carl went back in the house. The girls set the trap and tested it once. It worked like a charm. They reset the cage electronics and spread some dirt and grass over the bottom on the ground and looked at their experimental animal trap.

"I hope it's big enough to hold the animal," Roxy commented. "One last thing. We've got to make sure the switch is set to '*ON*'."

The girls watched the trap for about fifteen minutes before they tired of the boredom. Dexie looked at her watch, decided she had better return home, practice her clarinet for at least thirty minutes, and collect her school supplies.

"Bye Rox. Tomorrow at school you can tell me if you catch anything. I want to see what it is. Make sure you give it water and keep it warm. We don't want to have a dead creature," Dexie laughed.

"Okay sis, see you tomorrow."

Roxy sat on the steps and looked at the trap, her hands cradling her head. Some thoughts passed through her mind. "What if the trap goes off at night? There's no way for me to tell without coming outside to see if anything happened. I wonder if dad could put a little red light on the cage. That way I could see from my bedroom window if the trap closed. If the light goes out, something's in the trap. But the light could go out if the battery needs to be replaced. I'll have to make sure I have a backup battery."

Roxy's thoughts were interrupted by her mother's voice and sounds coming from the kitchen. The young detective could hear the dishwasher and decided she would ask if she could help her mom get dinner started. On Sunday, dinner was at four o'clock and afterward, the family watched TV and talked until around eight; exceptions were rare.

It was 8:15 when Roxy checked the trap but nothing had happened. She could still see the penny enticing some magical being to take it and get trapped in the cage. The next time she would check the apparatus was in the morning. Roxy sharpened some pencils and got some clothes ready for school. At ten o'clock she climbed into bed but couldn't go to sleep. She put on her slippers and went outside to check the trap one last time. Roxy pointed a flashlight beam on the penny.

The coin was still there, nothing had happened. Disappointed, Roxy went back in the house, locked the door and went to bed. As she slid under the covers, she said, "Maybe tomorrow," and closed her eyes.

Roxy woke up and glanced at her alarm clock. It was almost eight o'clock, Labor Day morning. She suddenly thought, "The trap!" Quickly dressed in jeans and sweatshirt, she stepped into her slippers, then ran down to the kitchen. The coffee maker was on, but no one was up yet. She opened the back door, looked down at the trap for the penny. It was gone, but the trap hadn't closed. Roxy stepped down to the driveway, eyes focused on the trap.

"Why didn't the trap work?" she questioned as she bent down to look at it more closely. The metal rod was lying on the ground outside the trap so the solenoid had been triggered. She could see a small stick holding the cage open and the penny was on the concrete at the bottom of the first step. "Hmm, what is going on? Time to have a talk with Dad!"

She turned the electronics off and went in the house after picking up the penny.

"Dad!" she yelled.

"Yes, Roxy, what is it?" Her dad was a couple of feet away pouring some coffee. "Not so loud, dear."

"I'm sorry, I didn't see you. The trap didn't close, but the penny was at the bottom step. There was a piece of tree branch keeping the cage from closing."

"I guess you're dealing with a pretty smart critter, Roxy. I think one of your friends is pulling tricks on you. No bird or other small animal I can think of would do that. We're going to have to get the big guns out now."

"What do you mean by big guns, Dad? You don't mean a weapon, do you?"

"No, dear. We're going to out-smart the penny magician! My digital camera is going into action and we'll get some digital movies of our mystery being. I'll set it up so the camera will take multiple shots when the solenoid fires. What do you think about that, detective Maxwell?"

"That's awesome, Dad. Really awesome!"

The holiday was very boring for Roxy. After lunch, she phoned Dexie, but Dex was busy doing something with her parents, so Roxy didn't have anyone nearby to hang out with. She cleaned her room, sat in front of her computer for an hour or so, and tried to imagine what was going on with the trap she and her dad had constructed. She had been positive it would give some results, but all that happened just created more questions.

Roxy shut off her computer and looked out her bedroom window for a few minutes. A light east wind was blowing, causing tree leaves to flutter and fall to the ground. She could see a bird's nest that she hadn't seen before, but it was not occupied. It looked like some eggshells were all that resided in the circular construction of twigs, mud, and grass. She wondered if occupants would come in the spring to raise a new family when the tree was again covered with large green leaves.

After selecting a book from the top of her clothes' cabinet and sitting down on the edge of her bed, she swung her feet up and leaned back against her pillow. She began reading page one of the novel and made it to page 3 before there were no more words or pages. Roxy had fallen asleep.

Roxy was watching the bird's nest in a big tree outside her window. Two birds were coming and going with pieces of grass and twigs, rebuilding and strengthening the nest after the winter ruin from cold winds and snowy weather. She noticed something shiny in the middle of the nest was reflecting the sun.

Binoculars would give her a better view so she got the field glasses from her closet and focused the lenses on the nest. The image was very clear, the shiny object was a coin, a dime. She looked closer and could also see a penny and a nickel. One of the birds flew off and returned a minute later with another penny. Roxy had never heard of birds collecting money. Where did they get the money and from whom?

A loud bang startled her—someone must be shooting at the birds.

"Roxy! What are you doing? Did you fall?" Her mom was checking on her after hearing the loud noise that came from upstairs.

Roxy sat up and looked around. Her book was on the floor. She had fallen asleep and the book had slid off the bed and crashed on the hardwood floor. "I'm okay, Mom. I just dropped a book."

"All right. You'd better get ready for dinner."

"Okay." She blinked her eyes a few times and went to the bathroom to wash. She looked in the mirror and brushed her hair as she thought, "That dream was so realistic!"

Chapter 5

First Day: Seventh Grade

oxy was up before dawn on Tuesday, the first day of a new school year. She had awakened before her alarm went off. At first, the coin mystery was only one thing on her mind. But then she got excited about having classes in a new building, having a locker with a combination lock, having new teachers, and instead of recesses, she would have a class of physical education, PE. She was especially interested in two new classes: her math class, algebra 1, and art class; her other classes were continuations of the usual subjects, like English and History.

She had washed her new jeans and softened them by wearing them in the house for several hours the night before. When she was dressed, she sprayed some of her mom's perfume in the air and walked through the nearly invisible cloud. She didn't want to overdo the scent the first day of classes.

As she slipped into her black flats, she heard her mom call, "Roxy, better get up. I'll have some eggs for you in a couple of minutes." She heard the downstairs bathroom toilet flush and her dad's steps going toward the kitchen. Her upstairs room was like a guard tower, she could tell where her parents were at all times unless they weren't wearing shoes. But most of the time she wasn't paying that much attention. She heard her dad slide a chair out from under the kitchen table and then the downstairs was quiet. Roxy grabbed her backpack and went down to the kitchen.

Carl looked up from his watch and said, "You've got about ten minutes, Rox. You'd better hustle, dear. Remember, the bus won't wait."

Roxy poured milk over some Cheerios and took the bowl up to the bathroom where she combed her hair and wolfed down the cereal. She ran back downstairs, drank some orange juice, grabbed her book bag and headed out the door. The bus stop was in front of Dexie's house where half a dozen kids were waiting. Roxy ran past three houses on her way to meet the bus. She didn't see Dexie but she did see Dean Walker, the fifth grader with dirty fingernails.

When the bus rolled to a stop and the red lights started blinking, the door opened and the kids started scrambling up the steps. Roxy was the last one to begin climbing into the big yellow bus when Dexie came running from her front door.

"Wait!" she yelled. Almost out of breath, her backpack swung from side to side as she ran. Roxy was happy to see Dex, she was almost late. The amateur detective had to tell Dexie about the latest trap incident and find out why Dex had nearly missed the bus. Her BFF was never late for anything.

Breathing hard, Dex sat down on the seat next to Roxy and sighed. She wore a frown and Roxy was dying to find out what happened. But Roxy didn't want to butt into Chappell family problems, so she kept her mouth zipped. She also didn't want to open her mouth for another reason. She had run so hard she felt like she might throw up, the taste of milk and Cheerios was in her throat.

Dexie sat quietly for a moment until her breathing was almost normal, and then she said, "My mother! She made me put my clarinet upstairs in my bedroom, so I had to take it up there and then come back downstairs, get my books, and run to the bus. I almost didn't make it!"

Roxy thought that Dex was making a bigger thing out of it than necessary but didn't respond. Roxy let a few more seconds pass while Dexie adjusted her book bag.

"Dex, I've got some news about the trap," she whispered.

"Oh! I was about to ask you if anything happened last night."

"Quiet, Dexie, not too loud. We don't want anyone to know what we're doing. They could mess it up," warned Roxy.

"Oh yeah, I guess you're right. So, what happened?" Dex murmured.

"The trap was set off, but a small piece of a branch kept the cage from capturing anything. The penny was at the bottom of the first step on the concrete, just like before. Dad thinks something other than an animal is messing with us. He's going to hook up his camera and get some pictures when the solenoid goes off."

"Hey girls! A penny for your thoughts!"

It was Dean sitting with one of his buddies across the aisle from Roxy and Dex. He had noticed the girl's whispering and wanted to find out what the secret was.

Roxy said, "Hi Dean. If you want our thoughts, it's going to cost you more than a penny! For you, about five bucks—no, ten."

Dexie started laughing and Dean replied, "Nothing you would say could ever be worth five bucks. Forget it!"

Dean and his buddy, Rudy, both laughed.

Dex poked Roxy and said, "Do you think he could be involved? He mentioned a penny."

"I don't think so. That was just a coincidence, a figure of speech," Roxy replied.

But Roxy knew some intelligence was behind the penny magic, but it couldn't be Dean. He wasn't blessed with a brilliant mind. He wasn't dumb, but she thought three digits in his IQ were not likely.

The bus breaks squealed as they stopped in front of the school. Kids started streaming off the bus, heading for their homerooms, resembling the haphazard traffic of a bunch of ants dropped on the ground. Dex and Roxy walked together to Mrs. Willet's room for English at the north end of the building. As they entered the classroom, Roxy said, "I'll talk to you later, Dex."

"Yeah, later," Dexie replied, gave a little wave of her hand, and smiled.

The best friends sat on opposite sides of the classroom so they couldn't talk again until the ten minutes between classes. They didn't want to risk passing notes, undoubtedly, someone would read them. The girls had decided to set as far apart as possible because they knew they would get in trouble for talking. Neither girl wanted negative comments on their report cards.

During PE, the girls were able to talk in whispers about Roxy's father setting up his camera to record whatever was messing with their penny. They were playing kickball and didn't have much of a chance to talk since they were on opposite teams. When one of the girls kicked the ball so hard it had to be chased they had a chance to talk.

"I've been thinking, Rox. What if it's a weird snake or something? That would be creepy!"

Roxy answered, "Or a salamander, or a mouse with two heads," she laughed. "It has to be something with hands to put the stick in place of the metal rod and able to pick up the penny, or roll it, I guess."

"Yeah, and what if there are more than one?" quizzed Dex.

"Jeez. I hadn't thought of that," Roxy remarked and then bit her lower lip. "What if these things got into the house? If they're like gremlins, they could cause all kinds of problems. But gremlins aren't real, are they? No, gremlins are imaginary! If it's a Lilliputian-sized animal, I hope it's cute like Tinkerbelle."

The next opportunity for the girls to talk occurred on the homeward bound bus, number 13; the same bus they had taken in the morning.

Dexie grasped Roxy's wrist, looked in her eyes and whispered, "I thought of something else, Rox. Could Lilliputians be doing the penny thing?"

"Aren't they imaginary, Dex, from Gulliver's Travels?"

"Yes. But something like that?" Dex replied. "You know, little people."

"I thought of that, too. But I was thinking it might be a gremlin, but they're imaginary too, and we're on bus 13—we've never had any problems," Roxy grinned. "I guess we'll have to wait and see what the pictures show us."

"When do you think your dad will have the camera set up?"

"Probably next weekend. He's been pretty busy at work and doesn't have much free time to play with his camera. I'll let you know when the camera is ready for action."

During the remaining time on the bus ride, Dex and Rox talked about the middle school cheerleading squad and whether they would try out. Roxy said she wasn't interested and Dexie was undecided. Both girls already had several activities that would keep them busy during the seventh grade, which had just started. After one day of school, they didn't have any homework, but what would happen by the end of the week? They could get very busy quickly; fall semester was full of school activities.

The girls stepped off the bus in front of Chappells'. Dex started toward the front door but spun around and ran to catch up with Roxy.

"Can I come home with you?" Dex asked.

"Sure, Dexie. You don't want to go in your house?"

"No one's home and you have a mystery to solve. I'd much rather work on a mystery than practice my dumb clarinet. Sometimes I hate that thing. I think this year I'll take a break from the band and try it again in eighth grade. Maybe I'll enjoy it more then, but Mom might not let me do that."

"Maybe you could join the science club with me, I know you like math. We could work on a project together and enter the science fair. But if you're a cheerleader, you probably won't have time for a science project. Boy, we sure have some tough decisions to make, don't we?"

As the best friends looked down the street toward the Maxwells' property, Roxy saw her dad's truck parked in front of the house at the curb.

"Hey, my dad is home early. I hope he didn't get fired!"

"Maybe he's working on the camera!" Dex suggested.

The front door was unlocked so the girls entered, dropped their books on the piano bench, and sauntered into the kitchen.

"Hi girls! Are you hungry? I've got some fruit pieces in that bowl on the table. Help yourselves."

Mary had been home from shopping for about fifteen minutes. She had to pick up a few things she had forgotten when she sent Carl and Roxy to the store on Sunday.

"Dad's out in the garage, dear. He's working with his camera. I think it's for your trap so you can photograph the animals."

Dex looked at Roxy, smiled, raised her right hand above her head and snapped her fingers. She had been right about Roxy's dad working on the camera.

Roxy pulled out the silverware drawer and selected two forks. She handed a fork to Dex and they attacked the fruit bowl with abandon. In less than a minute, fruit juice was dripping off their chins and onto the tabletop. Mary gave them each a paper towel so they could mop up the juice from the table and wipe their hands and faces.

Mary laughed and said, "I guess you weren't hungry."

"Oh, Mrs. Maxwell! That was so good! I'll have to come over more often."

"Yeah, Mom, the fruit was almost as good as the cake you made Sunday. Is there any cake left?"

"Sorry dear, your dad and I finished it off last night—after you went to bed."

"Thanks anyway, Mom. We've got to see what Dad is doing."

"Thanks, Mrs. Maxwell."

"You're welcome, girls. Here, give me those forks."

Mary reached out and the girls handed her the forks, then they went outside to the garage.

"Hi ladies! How was school today?"

"Oh, it was all right. How's the work on the camera coming, Dad, and why are you home so early?"

"I had a meeting that was supposed to last all afternoon but one of the contractors didn't show up so we finished early. That gave me a chance to come home and work on the camera. I'm almost ready to test it. You guys can be the animals," he grinned.

"Why don't you two take the trap and put it in the same place as before. I'll bring the tripod and camera."

Roxy and Dexie carried the trap out to the steps and set it up on the lawn with dirt and grass covering the hinged door. They pushed the nails through the corner holes to hold the cage in place and inserted a penny in the wire clips. Roxy remembered the metal rod this time.

Carl set the tripod up, attached the camera and wires and aimed it at the penny.

"All set! Roxy, flip the switch on, and Dex, pull out the penny."

Dexie reached into the cage with the needle nose pliers and grabbed the penny. When she pulled on the coin, the solenoid fired, the rod fell and the cage snapped shut on the pliers. Dex had remembered to let go of the pliers and remove her hand quickly. In addition to the solenoid firing, the camera took ten pictures in rapid succession.

"It worked, Dad!"

"Sure, it worked. Doesn't everything I build work?" He frowned as if the girls might think that his contrivance might not function. "Don't answer that!" Carl laughed.

"Show us the pictures, Mr. Maxwell! I want to see my fingers, especially my nails!" Dexie laughed.

"Dex, you are too funny!" Roxy laughed.

CAM

Chapter 6

Neighborhood Spy

As Dean walked home from the bus stop, he passed Roxie's house, across the street, three lots down from his ranch-style home at the corner. He watched as Dexie and Roxy went in the front door. Half-a-minute later, he punched in the code on the garage door to get into the house when his parents were both at work. His mom, Cynthia Walker, worked at the Western City Bank and would be home at four o'clock, or a few minutes after. She got off at 3:30 but had a twenty-minute commute and usually stopped to pick up something for dinner.

The garage door started up and Dean crouched so he could duck under it. He hustled over to the button at the door into the kitchen and pressed it. The noisy garage door stopped raising and started back down. He took a glance at his father's collection of WW2 firearms mounted on the garage wall on a sheet of painted plywood. The guns were all disabled so they couldn't fire, and besides, there wasn't any ammunition.

He changed his clothes in his bedroom and flopped back on the bed, staring at the ceiling and thinking, "Why are those girls always huddled together and whispering? Maybe if I sneak down the alley and take a look at Roxy's backyard I can find out what they're doing."

He started out the back door but then remembered the German sniper rifle in the garage. The old gun had a telescope on it, perfect for spying. He reversed his steps, went in the garage, and looked at that old gun. It was mounted so the only way to get it would be to take the whole display down and release the metal holders from the back. He looked at the scope and saw that it was attached to the rifle with four screws. All he needed was a small screwdriver!

Ten minutes later, he had the telescope off the gun with the four little screws stored in an old Band-Aid can. He set the temporary storage container on the top of his dad's workbench. When he returned from his mission, he would remount the scope. No one would ever know it had been borrowed. He knew that he should ask his dad if he could borrow the little telescope, but he would miss the opportunity to do some spying if he had to wait until his dad came home from work. He usually got home about 7:00 p.m.

Dean stuck the telescope in his pocket. Only a couple of inches stuck out. No one would even notice he had the scope. He left through the back door and locked it. When he got to the corner and crossed the street, he walked to the alley, made a left turn and made his way past the neighbors' garbage cans. The lid on Mrs. Thompson's can was not closed and flies were swarming around the opening. He moved across the alley from that container to avoid the bugs and the odor he expected to smell.

The fourth house down was the Maxwells' although Dean had to make sure. He had never looked at their house from the alley. It was the one with the chain-length fence and the thick shrubs on both sides of the gate that led to the garbage cans. The house next door to Roxie's belonged to the Andersons'. It had a telephone pole next to the garbage area. Dean stood behind the pole and sneaked a look into the Maxwells' backyard.

He duck-walked about ten feet where there was an opening between the gate and the fence pole—wide enough to stick the telescope through and watch what was going on. Dean pulled the telescope from his pocket and focused it on the girls near the kitchen porch next to the driveway.

"Hey you, boy! What are you doing?"

Dean was scared so much he almost wet his pants. He sat there looking across the alley at Mrs. Jeffers. She was holding a sack of garbage. It looked like the bottom of the sack was about to rip open. Something was dripping from the bag.

Dean couldn't think of what to say, so he stalled for time. He looked around and saw a bird, a robin, fly to the top of the telephone pole. He pointed up and said, "I'm bird watching. You scared the robin I was looking at. I was watching it pull a worm out of the ground."

"It looked to me like you were looking at someone in the Maxwells' yard."

"Oh, no ma'am, just a bird. The robin was on the grass in the backyard. It had a really big worm, about this long." Dean put down the scope and held his hands about six inches apart.

"Well, all right. But I don't want to see you spying on the Maxwell girl."

"No, ma'am. I wouldn't do that. She's too old for me anyway—I'm in fifth grade, she's in middle school."

Dean almost stood up, but he sat there until Mrs. Jeffers dropped her garbage in the can, took a last look at him, and went back in the house. Dean wondered if she was still watching him, so he took a quick look at the girls, noticed a device on the ground and a tripod. When he saw Mr. Maxwell, Dean got up and walked to the end of the block. He was sore at Mrs. Jeffers for messing up his camouflaged observation of Roxy and Dexie, but he had another idea.

Dean made a left turn, went to the corner, and made another left. He was only one house away from Roxy's place. He walked very slowly, looking to the left as he approached Maxwells' driveway. He heard Roxy say something about something working, but he couldn't see what had worked. So far, no one at the Maxwells' had seen him, so he continued down the sidewalk to the corner.

Dean crossed the street, went into the garage, reinstalled the scope on the sniper rifle, and went back to his bedroom. He sat on the edge of the bed thinking, "Spying is a lot harder than I thought. I'll have to try to listen very closely to what those girls are saying on the bus. I think I'll turn on the TV, set it on closed-captioned, the way grandma has it operating when she visits, and practice reading lips. One of the newscasters is usually on at this time."

Back at Roxy's, the detectives were unaware of Dean's spying. They were too occupied with their experiment and too far away to have heard Mrs. Jeffers talking with Dean.

"Let's look at the pictures. I want to see Dex's nails," Roxy grinned.

Carl removed the camera from the mount, pressed a couple of buttons on the camera and displayed the first picture. Dexie's fingers were a bit blurry since she had quickly pulled her hand away from the closing trap. The second picture showed the pliers on the ground with the penny lying near the metal jaws of the tool and the tips of Dex's fingers.

"Look, Dex! Your nails look great!" Carl exclaimed. "I guess we can't call you bad nails Dexie," he grinned.

Dex looked a little embarrassed and just smiled. The remaining pictures were identical. Carl decided the penny was a little hard to see in the photos so he gave Roxy a dime to put in its place.

After looking at all the pictures, Dexie suggested, "Dad, could you focus the camera on the cage with the dime in the upper right corner? That way we can see more of the opening. If the critter is still around, we might get more pictures of it close to the opening outside the cage."

"Now *that* is a good idea. You are becoming a very good analyst."

Carl refocused the camera. In order to keep it dry, he covered the camera with a grocery store plastic bag held in place with two rubber bands.

Carl stood up and announced, "Well, that should do it! Perhaps we'll have some pictures of the mystery guest tomorrow morning."

"Roxy, this is getting exciting! But I've got to get home or my mom will have a fit. I just remembered Mom asked me to vacuum the living room rug after school. See you in the morning! I hope something happens! Bye, Mr. Maxwell."

The girls went back in the house where they had dropped their backpacks. Dex hung her pack over her shoulder and they went to the front door and said goodbye. Roxy promised to show Dex any pictures of the mystery creature.

After dinner, Roxy checked the trap frequently, but nothing occurred up to her bedtime. Her mom was almost ready to tell Roxy to quit going outside, but Mary knew how important the mystery had become to Roxy and Dexie. It was nice to see the two girls so devoted to solving the coin conundrum. She was slightly worried the girls might become so involved they would get behind in their homework and their grades would suffer.

The phone rang at 10:00 p.m. It was Dexie. Roxy told her nothing had happened with the trap. She would see her tomorrow at the bus stop. Roxy climbed into bed, spent twenty minutes memorizing some vocabulary words, turned out her light and fell asleep.

Chapter 7

Success!

oxy's clock started buzzing at 6:45 a.m. She had set the alarm fifteen minutes earlier than normal, in order to give her plenty of time to check the trap and camera before getting ready for school. Roxy punched the off button, jumped out of bed and took a quick shower. Her school clothes were already in the bathroom so she almost finished getting ready for the day before going downstairs.

"Good morning, Mom," she sang the short greeting to Mary. Her mom was wearing a robe and slippers, making coffee and watching the morning news on a small flat screen installed in one of the upper kitchen cabinets.

"Good morning, Roxy. You must have lots to do today; you're already dressed for school. Do you want me to take you to school early?"

"No thanks, Mom. I just wanted to check the trap and camera to see if we have any pictures." Roxy went out the door, looked at the trap, and yelled, "It worked! We have some pictures! The dime is just where it should be, beside the bottom step."

She removed the plastic cover from the camera, released it from the tripod, and took it in the house. Roxy was afraid to try to look at the photos herself, fearing she might erase the evidence, so she yelled to her dad.

"Dad! Come and help me, please!"

Carl was rubbing his face and blinking his eyes as he walked slowly into the kitchen in his pajamas. Mary poured him a mug of steaming hot coffee and they all sat down at the table.

Roxy pushed the camera in front of her dad and said, "See if we have any pictures, please. Hurry, Dad! I'm dying to see what happened."

Carl took another sip of coffee, picked up the camera and said, "Get behind me, Roxy, so you can see what I see on each frame. You too, honey."

Mary moved her chair against Carl's so she could see the LCD screen. Roxy got up, moved behind her dad, put her arms around his shoulders and pressed her face next to his. Carl pressed a couple of buttons and the first picture was displayed.

Carl said, "Holy cow!"

"They're little people!" exclaimed Roxy.

Mary said, "I don't believe it! They're little green people. Oh, my gosh! The female is so cute!"

"Next one, Dad!" Roxy shook her dad, urging him to advance to the second picture. Carl swiped across the screen advancing to the next shot.

"Look, Dad! They're looking right at the camera and they're carrying the dime from the cage."

Mary said, "The boy's shorts look like they're made from woven grass."

Carl advanced to the next view.

"I can see the bigger one has his mouth open and the little one is looking right at it. They must be talking!" Roxy observed.

Carl advanced the camera to the remaining seven pictures, but nothing more could be seen of the little beings. He placed the camera back on the table and said, "Well, I'll be! We'd better keep this a secret or we'll have people trampling all over our yard and coming in the house. This place will be a mess and people will think we're crazy. The news media will have a field day."

"Dad, can you print the first picture for me so I can show Dexie?"

"Okay, but don't show it to anybody else. Remember, this must remain a secret. Tell Dexie she can't tell anyone, not even her parents—of course, they wouldn't believe her anyway."

"That's all right. Dex has lots of stuff she doesn't tell her mom and dad."

Carl stood and said, "I'll print the first picture for you."

Roxy looked at the kitchen clock and saw that it was 7:35 and she hadn't eaten anything yet. She practically drank her cereal, had a small glass of orange juice, grabbed her backpack and ran to the den. Carl handed her the picture as it was ejected from the printer and Roxy dashed out the front door headed for Dexie's and the bus.

As Roxy ran down the block, she rolled the picture into a tube and pretended it was a baton in a relay race. She had never run so fast before. Showing Dexie the picture was going to be so awesome! She couldn't get to the bus stop soon enough.

Roxy's heart was pounding when she arrived at the corner, not so much from the exercise, but from excitement. Dexie was waiting to climb on the big school bus. Dex had seen Roxy running and moved to the back of the line of students climbing the steps into the school vehicle.

Roxy took a couple of deep breaths to calm down and whispered, "Dex! They're little green people!"

"What?" Dexie nearly yelled, her eyes big as saucers.

"Yes! I have a picture! You've got to see this." She waved the rolled-up paper.

The girls climbed into the bus, moved about nine rows back and plopped down on a seat. They hadn't noticed that Dean was sitting behind them with his buddy, Jimmy Corbett, another fifth grader. Roxy began unrolling the picture and the girls huddled over it trying to prevent prying eyes from seeing anything. Dexie glanced across the aisle. The two students there were involved in a conversation of their own.

Dexie's head swiveled to check if they had an audience. "Okay, Rox, nobody can see. Show me the picture."

"Look! They're kind of cute, don't you think?"

"Jeez! Look at that!" Dex exclaimed as she pointed at the two little figures carrying the dime.

Suddenly a hand from behind them took the picture out of their hands. Dean had reached over the seat and grabbed the piece of paper. The girls turned around and both yelled, "Give that back!"

Dean was looking at the photo! Knowledge of the little people was no longer a secret unless the girls could react quickly.

"Looks like cartoon characters to me," Dean stated. "How'd you do that?"

Dexie decided to go along with it and said, "That's right. We're making a movie for a competition and we didn't want anyone to see what we're doing. Would you please give it back, Dean?"

"What's it worth to you?"

"Dean, does your father have a bank account at my dad's bank?" asked Dexie.

"What if he does?"

"Does your dad also have credit cards?"

"Sure. So?"

"What if your family started having trouble with their bank accounts and credit card payments? You might even get behind on your mortgage and lose your house. How would you like to be homeless and live in a car on the streets? Maybe you would have to move to another city or to the country and live on a debtor's farm. Do you think your parents would like that?"

"Okay. Here's your stupid picture."

"Thank you, you f-f-fifth grader!" Roxy acknowledged as Dean handed her the paper.

Dexie said, "Now sit back and keep your hands to yourself or you're going to have some real trouble and believe me, you don't want to find out what it is."

Dex turned to Roxy and said, "Wow, Rox, I thought you were going to say something really bad."

Roxy laughed and said, "I caught myself just in time. That was close! I almost lost it."

Roxy folded the picture and put it in her jeans' pocket out of prying eyes and grabbing hands. It would remain out of sight until Roxy was off the bus and walking home later in the day.

Chapter 8

Communications

The girls had decided to keep the paper out of jeopardy until they got home after school. When they got off the bus, Roxy waited for Dex to drop off her backpack and tell her mom where she was going. On the way to her house, Roxy succumbed to curiosity, took out the picture, unfolded it and looked closely at the little green figures.

"It looks like they're about four inches tall, about the height of the side of a shoebox," Roxy noted.

She handed the picture to Dex, who verified her observation, and said, "And look at their hands, they have a thumb and three little fingers. The little one's head is bald except for that little white flower. The boy has a full head of hair. Their ears look kind of like Spock's in Star Trek."

Roxy had been thinking about keeping the little people a secret.

"We need to have an explanation of what's in the pictures, Dex. Your idea of making a movie was a good one. We can say the little figures are made of clay and we made some tiny clothes out of grass and leaves."

"Okay. That sounds like a good plan. You need to show me the other pictures. You said you have two more, didn't you?"

"That's right. Dad probably printed all three of the pictures this morning. Mom will know where they are."

Mary was out at the curb removing the day's mail from the mailbox when the girls arrived. After their greetings, they went in the house.

"Mom, did Dad print the other two pictures after I left for school?"

"Yes dear. They're in the top right desk drawer in the den. He printed another of the one you took with you. He thought the one you had might get damaged if you carried it around all day."

"He got that right. I folded it up and put it in my pocket so no one else would see it."

"No one else?"

"Yes. We had to lie to Dean. We said it was a picture from a movie we are making. The little figures are made of clay."

Roxy informed her mother that Dean had grabbed it out of their hands and they had to threaten him to get it back.

"I almost called him a nasty name."

"Well, it's a good thing that it worked. But Mr. Chappell would never do such a thing. Besides, it would be against the law."

"Oh, we know that Mrs. Maxwell, but we had to get the picture back before Dean showed it to the whole school."

After looking at all three pictures, the girls had numerous questions about the little people. At the top of the list, they had made was how to communicate with the tiny green beings.

Roxy was looking at the picture showing the two little people seeming to be talking to each other.

"I'll bet their voices are hard for us to hear. We need to figure out how to hear what they say, if we can even understand their language. We need an amplifier."

"Hey, Rox, how about my karaoke machine? Do you think that would work?"

"Yes!" Roxy pumped her right fist. "That's awesome, Dex. What a great idea! But we'll also need a recorder."

"You know, this project is getting more and more complicated. If we have a bunch of equipment to observe the—the little green people, do you think we're going to scare them away?" Dex observed.

"I was thinking the same thing, Dex. We'll have to ask my dad if he can think of a way to conceal the equipment, like put it inside and use extension cords. Do you think we should change where the trap is located so the little people can discover the coin in a different place? Also, I've been thinking— we don't need the top of the trap, just the coin device to start the recording equipment, and the solenoid isn't necessary. We don't need to capture them. I think the noise of the solenoid might have startled the little people last time."

"Oh! I just had a brainstorm, Rox. What about using a video recorder? Can we ask your dad about that?"

"Jeez, Dex, you are full of good ideas. Where are your ideas coming from?"

"Maybe from all the books I've been reading." Dex raised her eyebrows and grinned. "I had a good night's sleep, too."

Roxy replied, "Me too, so I don't think sleep's the reason." Both girls started giggling.

Dex and Roxy sat on Roxy's bed with a notebook and wrote down some questions to ask the tiny beings. They had about twenty items on their list when Dex looked at her watch and said sadly, "Darn, I had better go home, it's after four o'clock."

"Hey, Dex, just a minute."

Roxy dropped the notebook on the bed, ran downstairs and came right back.

"Mom said it's all right if you stay for dinner. Call your mom and ask her if it's okay."

Dex went to her backpack, pulled out her cell phone and a minute later she said, "She said okay, but I have to be home at 7:00 p.m. I have to practice my clarinet and do some schoolwork. I've got some math homework. How about you?'

"I have study hall when you have band. I did my homework already."

Carl Maxwell returned home from work a little after 5:00 o'clock. Roxy and Dex were watching him as he got out of his pickup carrying a small cardboard box.

"Let's check out what Dad has in the box," Roxy suggested, so the girls went downstairs, eager to see what Carl had brought home.

He entered the house, beaming with anticipation of what the girls would say when he showed them the contents of the package.

"Look what I have, girls."

Carl unfolded the flaps of the box, reached in and retrieved a camcorder.

Roxy spoke first, "Awesome! Where did you get that, Dad?"

All Dex could say was, "Wow!"

"One of the guys I work with loaned it to me. He bought a newer model and doesn't use this one anymore. I told him you guys had a project for a video camera and he said we could use this one. Pretty cool, huh?"

The girls spoke in unison, "How does it work?" They looked at each other and laughed, realizing they were on the same wavelength.

Carl took the manual from the box and they sat down at the kitchen table after Carl gave Mary a hug and a peck on the cheek.

"What do you have there, dear?"

"You mean, besides my sexy lips?"

"Carl! I mean that thing you're holding."

"That, my dear, is a camcorder for the girls' little-green-people project. We're going to get action and sound from the magic little beings. We hope to communicate with them so we can get some questions answered, right girls?"

"Exactly, Mr. Maxwell," Dex seconded.

"Yeah, Dad. We have a big list of questions for them," Roxy announced.

"Well, let's start by learning how to operate this high-tech equipment." He laughed as he held up the instruction booklet. "I'll read the ten-year-old manual and you guys work with the camera."

Chapter 9

Questions

Thirty minutes later, the girls had a reasonable understanding of how to operate the camcorder, but they had to stop experimenting to eat dinner. As Dex and the Maxwells ate, they were consumed with talk about the little green people and how to use the camcorder. Carl feared the little people's voices would not be loud enough to be recorded but the girls told him they had planned to use Dex's karaoke machine as an amplifier.

"Dad, could we put the equipment in the house and use extension cords? Dex and I are afraid all the equipment will scare the little ones away. And can we remove the trap; we don't need to catch them. They aren't doing any harm."

"And they aren't ugly like moles," Dex contributed very seriously.

Carl smiled, gave a wink to his wife and said, "Sure, we can do those things. Good ideas, girls."

As soon as dinner was over, the investigation team planned their next experiment.

It seemed like they had just begun when it was seven o'clock and Dex had to return home.

Dex went to the kitchen and thanked Mrs. Maxwell for dinner. Roxy followed Dex to the front door and then decided to walk with her about half-way down the block. It wasn't getting dark until about 8:30 in middle September.

When they parted company, Dex said, "I'll see you tomorrow, Rox. I have to practice my clarinet now. Mom and I decided I should stay in the band." Dex pretended to stick her index finger down her throat and gag.

Roxy laughed and said, "See you tomorrow, sis," turned around and walked back home, only two houses away.

When Roxy got home she noticed the garage light was on, so instead of going in the house, she went in the garage. Her dad was busy working on the trap, removing the solenoid and cage from the section that held the coin mechanism. Roxy approached the workbench and said, "How are the amplifier and camcorder going to work?"

"I'm going to have two circuits, each one activated by a coin being removed as in our previous setup. When the first coin is removed, the amplifier and camcorder will be switched on and when the second coin is removed, the recorder playback will come on so you can ask them some questions. You and Dex will have to record your questions for them and give them some time to answer each question. You might start out by telling them you will not hurt them; you just want to find out who they are."

"Awesome, Dad. Dex and I will record some things tomorrow after school. When can we try it out?"

"I should have it ready by Thursday. We'll have a dry run tomorrow evening. Okay?"

"Good! I'll tell Dex tomorrow on the bus. Thanks, Dad." Roxy pulled her dad's arm down and gave him a kiss on the cheek.

"I'll never wash that spot again, Roxy," Carl smiled.

"I don't believe you, Dad! You'll probably get some kind of infection if you don't wash," Roxy giggled. "You'll scratch off your whiskers and then you'll have a bald spot on your cheek."

Roxy was up, dressed, and ready to eat breakfast before her parents had gotten up. She was excited about telling Dex the new plans for Wednesday evening. She was one of the early members of the gathering group of children waiting for the bus when Dex came out of her house and walked slowly toward the bus stop.

Roxy couldn't help noticing Dex's demeanor. Dexie almost looked sick.

"Are you all right, Dex?" Roxy inquired.

Tears were forming in Dex's eyes and she said disappointedly, "I can't come over after school today. I have to do my homework and practice my clarinet before my dad gets home. He doesn't want me to play it when he's home. I'm so sorry, Rox."

"That's okay, Dex. You can come over after dinner, can't you?"

"I guess. Will that be all right?"

Dex wiped her eyes and Roxy put her arm around Dex's shoulder.

"Sure, it will only take us a few minutes to get the tape recorder ready and then we'll get everything set up. Dad won't mind, he'll have another cup of coffee and some more dessert while we wait for you," Roxy smiled. "Maybe I'll get him to walk around the block with me instead of having more dessert. I want him to be around when I have kids so Mom and Dad can babysit for me."

"You're planning pretty far ahead, Rox," Dex smiled.

The bus ride to school was filled with whispers as the girls planned the questions to ask the little people.

After dinner that evening, Roxy, her mom, and dad went for a walk and passed by the Chappells' house and turned toward home. Dex ran out to meet them and the foursome walked down the street to the Maxwells'.

Carl asked, "Have you guys got your questions ready?"

Roxy answered, "Uh-huh. We're ready to record the questions, right Dex?"

"Uh, almost ready. I have a couple more things to consider. I wrote them down so I wouldn't forget." Dex gave Roxy a piece of folded paper and Roxy read the questions.

"Oh! That's a good one, Dex." Roxy read, "Where did you come from?"

When they reached the Maxwells', Mary excused herself and went to clean up the kitchen; the girls and Carl went to the garage. A piece of notebook paper with Roxy's questions was fished from her pocket and the girls recorded a message for the little people to not be afraid and then asked questions with pauses for the answers.

Carl listened to what the girls had asked and was in complete agreement so he finished the wiring and was ready for a test run. This time they were using four coins, two pennies, and two dimes. Carl explained to the girls that he wanted to see if the color of the coins made any difference in the order of them being moved. He also wanted to use four coins to keep the little people around longer.

Carl and the girls tested the apparatus, made some sound level adjustments and set up their experimental equipment a little farther from the steps than before. Medium length cords were

necessary to reach the outdoor electrical box. Carl borrowed some outdoor extension cords stored with Christmas decorations so they didn't have to buy anything. Except for the camera, he had put everything in a big, dark-green, plastic container against the house next to the steps.

The girls checked everything twice before they went in the house.

"I sure hope this works, Rox."

"Me too. It's just like Christmas Eve when I was little and we were waiting for Santa Claus to deliver our presents! I'm so excited to see if we can communicate with them. I bet I'll have trouble going to sleep tonight."

Dean had been scouting near the Maxwells' before his dinner; his father was going to be home around 7:30 and it would take him about twenty minutes to clean up, so Dean and his parents would be eating at 8:00 p.m., not an unusual time for the Walker family. He had sneaked down the alley behind Roxy's place, but couldn't see much, so he walked to the end of the alley, turned left and walked past the Chappells' to his side of the street, made another left and walked slowly, humming as he sauntered down the sidewalk.

As he passed the Maxwells' residence, he saw Dexie and Roxy going in the house. Dean sat on the curb for about ten minutes before the front door opened. Dean quickly moved behind Mrs. Trimble's big shrub and observed Dexie come out and head home. All Dean heard was "See you on the bus tomorrow." Dean decided the activity was over, so he waited a minute for everyone to go inside and went home.

When Dean got in the house, his dad was taking a shower, so he went in the kitchen and asked if his mom needed any help. She said no and asked if he had washed his hands. Dean looked at his hands, saw that his fingernails were dirty, and went in the hallway bathroom. As Dean washed, he decided to ask his dad if he could borrow the telescope that was on the sniper rifle. He dried his hands and looked at his fingernails. They were still dirty. He was going to use a scrub brush on them tomorrow.

During dinner, there was a break in his parents' conversation.

"Dad, could I use the sniper rifle telescope?"

There was silence for a moment as his dad looked at him and then at his mom. There wasn't any response of any kind from his mom, she just kept chewing.

Dean looked at his dad, thinking, "What if he says 'No'?"

"I guess it would be all right. What are you going to look at?"

Dean was surprised and almost lost control of his fork. "Uh, the moon."

"Yeah. I noticed as I was coming home, there's almost a full moon. But that telescope isn't very powerful; you might not be able to see any craters."

"I just want to try, Dad."

"Okay, I'll help you take it off that old gun. You want it tonight?"

Dean nodded and said, "Uh-huh, but I can take it off. I don't want to bother you after you worked so hard all day."

"Well, okay. There's a screwdriver in the top bench drawer—on the left."

"Thanks, Dad."

"Don't go around looking in windows. You hear?"

"I won't, Dad."

Dean went out the back door and over to the alley leading to Roxy's. When he arrived at the gate to Roxy's backyard, he crouched down, took out the telescope and looked at the moon. The light coming through the lenses was very bright so he decided to forget about the moon. That wasn't his first choice to observe anyway. He had to find out what the girls were up to. The moon didn't supply enough light for Dean to see what was on the ground near the kitchen porch.

Dean opened the gate slowly to avoid any noise and slipped through the opening, crouching as low as possible. He made his way along the garage until he was close to the area the girls had occupied earlier. The moonlight was bright enough so he could see some coins on the ground. He got closer and saw two dimes and two pennies.

The next thing he did was a big mistake! He dropped to his knees and reached for the dimes and pennies. They were stuck to something, so he gave a little tug and they came loose. He heard a whirring noise and then Roxy's voice saying they wouldn't be hurt. Roxy's voice seemed loud enough so someone in the house might hear her. There wasn't time for Dean to listen to any more of Roxy's voice. He had to get out of there! Dean ran as fast as he could to get away from the Maxwells' house.

Out of breath when he got home, Dean went in the back door and into the garage to put the telescope back. He reached for it and looked down at his pockets. The telescope was gone!

He figured he must have dropped it when he sneaked into Roxy's backyard. He stood there thinking, "Should I risk going back for the telescope? If they find it in the grass, they won't know who it belongs to, but I have to get it back. It's Dad's."

Dean went back outside and retraced his steps to the alley gate at the Maxwells'. Most of the backyard was in shadow, so he dropped to his hands and knees and began crawling and searching in the grass for the telescope. The garage light came on and he froze for a moment and then rolled into the garage's shadow for safety.

"Who's out there?" It was Mr. Maxwell's voice!

Dean stopped breathing, frozen in place. Then he heard Mr. Maxwell again.

"Who's in the backyard? I'm warning you, get out of my yard or I'm coming back there with a baseball bat."

Dean let out his breath, gulped another, and stayed on the ground. He waited about a minute, but it seemed much longer, and the light went out. Dean heard the kitchen door close.

He waited another minute or so, assumed Mr. Maxwell had gone back inside, and he crawled back to the gate. One more step and he would be out of Maxwells' yard. His knee hit something hard and he felt in the grass with his left hand. It was the telescope! Dean put the scope in his pocket, slithered through the opening in the gate, closed the backyard entrance with hardly a sound, and ran the length of the alley as fast as he could go.

As Dean entered the back door, his mom called out, "Dean, you'd better stay inside now, people in cars can't see you very well at night."

"Okay, Mom."

Dean put the telescope back on the rifle and went to his room. After he had his shoes and jacket off, he was still breathing hard. He lay on his bed and tried to relax, but his heart was still pounding away as if he had just run a quarter mile. It was time for analysis. Dean began to think, "Why was Roxy saying she wouldn't hurt someone? Why did she ask where they were from? Who were *they*?"

It suddenly popped into Dean's mind, "Those figures in that picture I saw on the bus must be real, and not models made of clay!"

Chapter 10

It Works!

oxy finally went to sleep about midnight. She had tried counting sheep, putting everything out of her mind, and listened to songs on her iPod shuffle, but nothing seemed to work. Finally, she removed the shuffle's earplugs, turned off the iPod and drifted off to sleep. Roxy was in a vegetable garden talking to a big green pea when her alarm went off and she sat up in bed, startled by the noise. It was a gray Thursday morning.

She wiped her face with her hand, swung her legs out of bed and sat there for about a minute. She looked at her clock. The big red LEDs said 5:31 a.m. She had set her alarm a half hour earlier than normal. It was time to check the apparatus to find if the attempt to communicate with the little ones had been a success. She slid her feet into her slippers and pulled on her bathrobe as she descended the steps to the living room and hurried through the kitchen. As she opened the door she noticed her slippers were on the wrong feet, pinching her big toes, but she didn't care. More important things had to be taken care of.

Roxy looked for the coins, they were all missing. She wondered, "What happened to the coins?" Nothing had been moved to the concrete at the edge of the grass. She checked the circuit again and the coins were gone. Roxy was excited, but puzzled, too. She almost couldn't think of what to do next. She took a deep breath, let it out slowly, released the camcorder from its mounting, and took it in the kitchen.

Her mom was making coffee and asked, "Did it work, dear?"

"I think so, Mom. I just have to remember how to play back the recording. I'd better get the manual so I don't erase anything. Do you know where Dad put the manual?"

"I think he left it on the coffee table in the living room."

Mary watched Roxy walk into the living room and said, "What's wrong with your feet, dear?"

"Oh, nothing. I put my slippers on the wrong feet when I got up," she tittered.

Roxy kicked off her slippers and put them back on correctly, grabbed the instruction manual and returned to the kitchen, reading as she walked. Roxy found "playback" and was reading as she pulled a chair back from the table and sat down.

Carl, in bare feet, tee shirt, and pajama pants, had joined Roxy at the table.

"I think someone was outside last night, Rox. I looked out there but didn't see anyone. I think someone triggered the recorder, but it wasn't the little beings."

"But, Dad, who would be out there in the dark?"

"Let's see if we got an intruder with the camcorder."

Mary handed Carl a mug of steaming hot coffee and poured Roxy some orange juice. Mary filled her coffee mug, added a teaspoon of milk and joined Carl and Roxy to see the show.

Roxy said, "Here goes!"

Two human hands were holding the dimes and pennies. They moved out of view. Nothing else important was on the recording. It had only recorded the two hands and the shiny coins. Sounds of someone running could be heard on the audio.

Roxy played back the recording and stopped it when the hands appeared, taking the dimes and pennies.

"Dad! I know who that is! Look at the brown skin and dirty fingernails! That's Dean! Boy, is he gonna get it."

"Now, take it easy, Roxy. He still doesn't know what's going on. All Dean knows is that we put twenty-two cents on the ground and a recorder came on." Carl took a sip of coffee and continued, "Do you think you want him to know more?"

"I'm gonna tell him to give back the twenty-two cents and to stay out of our yard, and if he keeps coming around, his parents are going to know about it."

Dexie and Roxy got on the bus after all the other children at the stop had climbed on. They spotted Dean, sitting by himself, and sat down on the empty seat behind him. Roxy leaned over and poked Dean in the back. When he turned around, Roxy said, "You owe me twenty-two cents, bub."

"What twenty-two cents?"

"I've got a recording of your hands taking two dimes and two pennies from my yard. The coins weren't for you."

"Oh, the dimes and pennies for the little creatures—those coins? I'll give the money to you if you tell me about the little people you are trying to talk to. I heard the questions you were asking. You don't know much about them, do you?"

Roxy and Dexie whispered for a moment and Dexie said, "If you don't tell anybody about the little people, we'll let you help us investigate. What do you think? Otherwise, my dad will have to review your parents' accounts at the bank. No telling what will happen then."

Dean thought for a moment and nodded, "Okay. I'll come over after school today."

Roxy stuck out her hand, "It's a deal. Shake on it."

Dexie had dropped her books off and joined Dean and Roxy as they walked slowly down 23rd Place. Dean had joined the two girls as they started toward Roxy's house. He was full of questions. Most of them couldn't be answered by the girls; they didn't know enough about the little green beings. When they got to Roxy's house, he was still inquiring.

"So, when did you find out pixies were in your yard?"

"I don't think they're pixies, Dean." Dexie sounded like she knew what she was saying.

"I'm calling them pixies until we discover what they are." Dean was insistent.

Roxy answered, "Last Sunday we first noticed something was going on. We've been trying to figure out how to talk to them since we got pictures of them. We might have succeeded if you hadn't interfered."

"Sorry—but I wondered what you were whispering about. I was curious, so I started spying. But I didn't find out much until I took those coins and heard your questions. That's when I figured the little beings must be real. Your dad almost caught me. He really scared me."

Dexie and Roxy showed Dean all the equipment and got it ready for Friday morning. There wasn't much else to do, but they sat on the porch and talked for about ten minutes. Roxy promised she would let Dean and Dexie know what was recorded when she saw them in the morning on the bus.

It was still dark in the morning when Roxy got up. She got ready for school and sat downstairs waiting for dawn's light so she could see what the equipment had recorded. The coins were at the bottom of the steps, so she knew the little ones had been at work during the night.

"What are you doing, Roxy? It's cold outside. Come in and have some breakfast."

"Okay, Mom. I'm getting the camera. The coins have been moved, so we should have some new facts." Roxy brought the camera into the kitchen and sat down at the little side table.

She pressed two buttons and the camera flickered and started playing. The foldout screen showed the two little people, a little startled, looking at the camera and then bowing when Dex's voice told them not to be afraid, they wouldn't be harmed.

Their voices were high pitched and squeaky, the larger one spoke first and the smaller followed by repeating the last few words, subdued, almost like an echo.

"We from Nihon koku—Japan, *Nihon koku—Japan*."

Both little figures nodded and bowed toward the camera.

The larger one, the male, said, "We Niffits, *we Niffits*."

The larger one pointed at his chest and said, "Akira, *Akira*." He then pointed at the smaller Niffit and said, "Masako, *Masako*." The littler Niffit bowed and said, "*Masako*," and pointed a finger at her chest.

"Help humans is our duty, *our duty*. Find things and return them, *return them*."

"Put circles so you find, *you find*. So not lose, *not lose*."

"Want go home, *go home*, to Nihon koku, *Nihon koku*."

The next to last question the girls had asked was "How did you get here?"

Akira answered, "Big water—tsunami, *tsunami*."

Masako stepped next to Akira, grasped his hand and said, "*Afraid we only Niffits here. Can help?*"

The last question from the girls was "Can we talk to you in two days—in the morning?"

The Niffits looked at each other, then at the camera, nodded and bowed.

Akira said, "Maybe we like that, *like that*."

Akira held up his tiny hand, put two fingers in the air and they disappeared into the grass.

Mary said, "We have to help them, but not right now, Roxy. You only have fifteen minutes to get ready for school."

"Tomorrow is Saturday and on Sunday we'll talk to the Niffits. This is so exciting, it's awesome!"

Roxy put two pieces of bread in the toaster, pushed the lever down and ran upstairs. She came back to the kitchen fully dressed, except for shoes, just as the toast popped up. She lathered a thick layer of strawberry jelly on her toast and stuffed it in her mouth as fast as it would go. Her cheeks bulged out as she poked the last bit of toast in. She took three chews, swallowed hard and washed it down with some skim milk.

Roxy wiped her mouth with the back of her hand and ran upstairs for her shoes, came back down to the living room, grabbed her book bag and was out the door.

"See you later, Mom and Dad."

Mary shook her head, grinned and said, "Wow, what a whirlwind! I hope she doesn't get a ticket for speeding."

Carl laughed and said, "Can you imagine what she's going to tell Dexie and Dean? I've never seen her so excited."

Carl was sitting at the table finishing his breakfast when Mary stepped behind him, rested her hands on his shoulders and said, "What if Roxy and Dexie want to take the Niffits home to Japan? And then there's Dean, he's new to the group."

Carl looked up at his wife, put his hands on hers and said, "Let's wait and see what they come up with. Maybe it won't come to that, but if it does, we'll have to figure out if we can send one of the girls to Japan. Hopefully, Dex's parents will cooperate and share the expenses. What do you think?"

Mary replied, "Well, let's see what the team comes up with after the Sunday talk."

Chapter 11

Trip to Japan?

It was 3:42 p.m. when the girls arrived at Maxwells'. Mary was reclining in Carl's chair reading a magazine when the girls came in the house. She was drowsy and had nearly fallen asleep. The noisy girls opening the front door brought her out of her lethargic feeling.

"Hi, Mrs. Maxwell! Did you see the Niffits answering our questions?"

"Hi Dexie. Yes, I sure did. We watched the video this morning. I'll bet you are excited. How was your first week of the seventh grade?"

"Oh fine. We had a normal day of classes, but I don't remember much. All I could think about was the Niffits."

"Mom, Dean's coming over in a few minutes. Do we have some cookies? He's always hungry. He said his dad comes home late from work so dinner is delayed."

"Sure. I can make some cookies. They're always better when they're hot from the oven. Funny, the Niffits sounds like a TV show. How about chocolate chip, or maybe peanut butter?"

"Not peanut butter, Mom. I think Dean said he's allergic to peanuts."

"Oh, I didn't know that. We'll make chocolate chip, about three dozen, so your dad will have something to munch on."

"Dex and I, too, Mom."

"Well, I guess four dozen then. I'll get started while you gals watch your Niffit matinee," Mary grinned.

"You and Dexie can stir in the chocolate chips but it will be a few minutes."

Roxy picked up the camcorder from the living room coffee table and Dex joined her at the dining room table. As the replay started, Roxy made a comment, "Listen to their squeaky voices, it sounds like an echo, but it is the little one repeating what the bigger one says. The bigger one's name is Akira and the smaller one is Masako. I think they are husband and wife."

Dexie watched and listened intently and seemed mesmerized by the actions and speaking of the little people. At the end of the recording, Dex just stared at the screen. Roxy didn't know if Dex was in a trance or just lost in thought.

Dex suddenly turned her head away from the camcorder screen, looked at Roxy and said, "We've got to help them get back to Japan, Rox! What can we do?"

"Girls, I need your help now," Mary spoke from the kitchen.

The doorbell rang and Roxy ran to the front door to let Dean in. He followed Roxy into the kitchen and said, "Hey, Mrs. Maxwell, baking cookies?"

"Yes, Dean. Pull up a chair and the girls will show you the recording of the Niffits. It will be about fifteen minutes before the cookies are ready."

Mary set the oven on 375 and began mixing the dough. The girls showed Dean the recording of the Niffits answering the questions. When the movie ended, Dean sat back and closed his eyes.

"Boy that smells good, Mrs. Maxwell. When will the cookies be ready to eat?"

Mary looked at her timer and said, "About five minutes, Dean. You must be hungry."

"Yes, ma'am. I forgot to take my lunch money today, but I had a piece of candy in my pocket."

"You should have eaten something when you got home."

"I thought about it, but I didn't want to miss out with the Niffits."

"Two more minutes, Dean. But you'll have to wait for them to cool."

Mary was preparing a second cookie sheet for the oven when she asked the girls to make another batch of dough for two-dozen more cookies. As they mixed the chocolate chips into the dough, the three ladies and Dean discussed the plight of the Niffits. How would they get the two little people back to Japan? The Niffits would have to pass through the scanners at the airport without being detected and keep out of sight for the duration of the flight across the Pacific. Dean was thinking of something else, not related to traveling.

The timer went off and the first dozen cookies were placed on a rack to cool. Dean came over and stood by them, only half-listening to the conversation.

As the second dozen cookies were being baked, Dexie came up with an idea.

"Tell me what you think about this. What if one of us, say Roxy, gets a ticket to Japan and passes through the scanners? I would make a paper airplane decorated with different colors, but lots of green, and saying "*Have a nice trip*!" The Niffits would be attached to the airplane and I would toss it to Roxy. She would catch the paper airplane, scoop up the Niffits and put them in her pocket. A TSA guard would probably grab the airplane from Roxy and open it but would only find "Have a nice trip!" written on the paper and throw it away. Guards might grab me too, but I wouldn't have anything on me, so they would let me go after telling me to never do that again."

"That sounds awesome, Dex. How did you think of that?"

"I was watching Johnny Withers make a paper airplane to send a note to his sister. They're in the same English class with me. When I was thinking of the problem with putting the Niffits through a scanner, I thought about the airplane. We could fly them into the boarding area," Dexie explained while grinning. "Do you think it would work? We can try it here first and get it down perfectly before we do it for real."

"I should throw the airplane. That's kind of a boy's activity, don't you think? Besides, there would be two catchers."

Mary said, "That's a wonderful idea, Dean. You three would make good detectives—or criminals! I hope you only use your ideas for good things! I wouldn't want to be visiting you guys in the penitentiary."

Mary, the girls, and Dean all laughed.

"That was a good one, Mom."

Mary noticed Dean was fidgeting near the cookies, so she said, "Dig in, Dean. I'll get you all some milk to drink."

Dean took two cookies, sat down at the table, and let out a big sigh. Roxy and Dexie were watching him and Roxy said, "A real cookie monster!"

"You bet! I could eat the first dozen all by myself!" Dean was stuffing the last morsel of the first cookie in his mouth.

That statement caused the girls to each grab a cookie and join Dean at the table.

Dean had started on the second helping when Mrs. Maxwell gave each detective a large glass of milk. Dean drank about half and came up for air. He licked his lips and said, "What are the Niffits going to when it gets cold? Do they have warm clothes? Where do they live during the winter?"

Roxy said, "Is that what you've been thinking about, Dean?"

"Yep. I was wondering if they would like to live in my sister's old dollhouse. Grace is in college now and she won't ever play with dolls anymore."

Dexie replied, "That sounds like a good idea, Dean. You are pretty thoughtful—and smart."

"I like that idea, too. But they would need heat, wouldn't they?" Roxy looked concerned.

"How about using a lightbulb? Your dad would have to put something over the back. It's open to the air." Dean was filling in the details of the miniature house.

"I'll ask Dad about it when he gets home tonight. On Sunday we'll ask the Niffits if they want to practice flying on a paper airplane, but first, we have to figure out how to get the money for the trip. Do you think your mom and dad would help pay for the ticket, Dex?"

"I don't know, Rox. We'll have to tell them about the Niffits and show them the video of the little people. My parents won't believe it at first. I bet they'll think we are trying to trick them—unless your mom and dad go with us when we show them the evidence."

Mary said, "We can do that, Dexie. Let's find out how much a round trip ticket to Japan would cost. Girls, why don't you check the Internet? Do you know how much a ticket to Japan would cost, Dean?"

"Nope. Sorry Mrs. Maxwell. I've never even been out of Oregon."

Roxy went to the computer and checked round-trip fares to Japan from Portland, direct flight. They didn't want to have to go through security more than once. Her search revealed a price of about $1,600 per person. When Dex and Roxy saw the amount, they were shocked and began to think the cost would make the plan out of the question.

"Mom! The price of one ticket is sixteen hundred dollars! That's if I just went alone."

Mary reacted, "That's not going to happen. You can't go alone. I'll have to go with you, or you don't go. We have some money in our emergency fund. I think this qualifies as an emergency."

Dex said, "Do you think we could find someone going to Japan and they could take the Niffits?"

Roxy said, "Another good idea, Dex. We can check church groups, libraries, universities, and government agencies to see if anybody is going to Japan on a tour or for business. But, I hate having to tell more people about the Niffits. I wanted to keep it a secret—just between our families. The fewer people that know about the little people, the better. We need to find out when the Niffits would like to travel."

"Gosh! It's almost five o'clock. I'd better get home and ask Mom if I can come over on Sunday. I'll see you tomorrow, Rox. Bye, Mrs. Maxwell! Bye, Dean."

Roxy escorted her BFF to the front door and waved as Dex started running down the sidewalk.

Carl got up at 7:30 Saturday morning. He was greeted by a gray sky and a misty rain. Mary, already making breakfast, heard the shuffle of his slippers as he approached the kitchen. Mary joined Carl at the table and said, "How are we going to get the Niffits back to Japan, dear?"

"I've been thinking about that. Our emergency fund isn't big enough to get all of us to Japan. If we go, I'd like all three of us to travel and stay a week or so. We can make it a real vacation. But we don't know when the Niffits want to go. Let's visit with Karen and Bruce Chappell tomorrow after the kids have talked to the little people. We'll go over in the evening and see what they think. We can show them the recording on the camcorder and tell them we don't have the funds for a trip to Japan."

Carl got up, refilled his coffee mug and grabbed a cookie.

"Hey! I made eggs and bacon for you. They're on the stove."

Carl grinned, "When you leave cookies out in the open like that, dear, I'm not responsible."

"Good morning!" Roxy was dressed, except for slippers. She grabbed a cookie and sat at the table.

"Good morning, Roxy. Like father, like daughter. Cookie monsters! Roxy, you and your dad should eat bacon and eggs. Cookies are not a good way to start a day. They don't last."

Roxy swallowed and commented, "I think Dean will be over today. He's going to bring over his sister's dollhouse." She looked at her dad and said, "Dean thought you could cover up the back and install a light bulb so the little house would have heat during the winter."

"He's coming over this morning with the dollhouse?"

"I think so. I'll call him and see when he'll be here."

"I've got some shingles we can put on the roof to make it waterproof. I'll have to see what it's made of before I put electricity in it. We can use an old set of outdoor Christmas lights to warm it up."

"I knew you'd have some good ideas, Dad. What would I do without you?"

"Your mom and you would do it yourselves or hire someone, or you'd bring the Niffits in the house." Carl thought for a moment, shook his head, and said, "No, that's not a good idea. Someone would step on them. They should stay outside."

Roxy phoned Dean. He said he would be over in about ten minutes—with the dollhouse.

Dean was prompt. There was a knock at the kitchen door. Mary glanced out the window and said, "Dean's here. He has the dollhouse in a wagon."

It was raining steadily now, so Roxy slipped on her raincoat and went outside. Water was dripping down Dean's forehead onto the steps.

"In the garage, Dean. I'll get the door for you." Roxy ran to the garage door and flung it open. Dean pulled the wagon with its cargo through the door and out of the rain. Roxy pulled the door closed and flipped on the lights.

The dollhouse was covered with a piece of canvas to protect it from water damage. They rolled the covering back and folded it. Roxy walked around the wagon eyeing the little house. She thought all the furniture and the dolls had been removed until she saw a bag stuffed into the miniature living room. Dean pulled it out and showed her the doll furniture.

"Think they'll like the furniture?"

"I hope so. I don't know what they have where they've been living. It should be better than leaves, dirt, and twigs. But maybe they like what they have. We can let them chose."

"I've been thinking, Roxy. What do they do about cats and dogs?"

Roxy glanced at Dean and replied, "I wonder. We'll have to ask them."

"Mom told me to come right back. I have to go to the church with her for choir practice. We're part of a presentation tomorrow. Bye, Roxy. I'll check with you tomorrow afternoon."

"Okay. Thanks for bringing over the dollhouse. Bye."

Chapter 12

Clothes and Conference

Sunday morning Roxy and Dex talked about meeting with the Niffits. Dexie had come over to the Maxwells' for breakfast. She had brought a small cardboard box with her which she put on the entry-way table. They didn't have to wait for Dean because he was busy at the Baptist church putting on his robe and getting ready to sing in the choir. Dexie was relating something she had heard her mother say on the phone, apparently about someone's birthday.

"My mom said, 'I think Botox didn't work.' That's all I heard. I don't know who she was talking to. I guess I shouldn't repeat it, but I know you won't say anything. I think she was talking to my aunt Janis."

"My mom tells me to go upstairs or go outside when she has calls like that." Roxy then said, "Let's go upstairs, Dex."

Dexie announced, "I want to show you something, Rox," as they entered Roxy's bedroom and sat on the bed. Roxy's eyes were focused on the box Dexie was carrying. She had no idea what might be in the box, but at the last second, before the box was opened, she thought it might be full of letters from some boy. She wished she had x-ray vision, but that would spoil Dexie's surprise.

"Here is what I wanted to show you."

Dex lifted the cover of the box and tossed it aside. Dex put the box on the quilt so Roxy could see what she had. The small cardboard box was full of tiny clothes and blankets Dex had made for the Niffits. Underneath the garments were little green dolls just the size of the tiny visitors.

"Gosh, Dex. These are awesome!"

Roxy put her arms around Dex and gave her a big hug.

"When did you have time to make these?" Roxy inquired as she inspected the miniature clothes and the little dolls.

"Last week. I gave up reading for a while," Dex smiled. "We can give them the tiny outfits when we talk to them. What do you think?"

"I think that's an awesome idea, Dex. I want you to see the dollhouse Dean brought over this morning. It's in the garage."

"Okay. I'll bring the box of clothes."

As Roxy went downstairs, with Dexie following, she thought of how organized Dex was and how, in contrast, she was so disorganized, except for her detective work. But she rationalized that, since she had numerous interests, if she took the time to get everything organized, she wouldn't have enough time for her many projects. That was her punishment for having an inquiring mind.

As the girls reached the garage, Roxy thought, "Why didn't I think of making the Niffits some clothes? Is Dexie a better person than I am?" She wondered if putting colored tags on her projects would help her keep things organized, but she decided that wouldn't work any better than keeping a written list. She had to talk to her mother, maybe later, after Dexie had returned home.

Dexie investigated the dollhouse and the miniature furniture for a couple of minutes before Roxy asked, "Shall we wait for them on the back porch? I hope they come soon, it's almost nine o'clock."

"I'm glad you came over when you did. I'd be very nervous by myself. Here, Dex, take the karaoke equipment and set it up at the corner of the house near where we had the trap. I've got the camcorder. Do you have your questions?"

"Slow down, Rox. We don't even know if the Niffits are coming. Where is the extension cord for the karaoke machine?"

Roxy let out a big sigh and yawned, not from lack of sleep, but from nervousness.

"You're right, Dex. I need to slow down." Roxy took a deep breath. "The cord is curled up beside the steps. It should still be plugged in, just uncoil it. Let's turn on the amplifier and sit down on the grass. We won't look so big that way."

Dexie looked at the grass and stated, "The grass is wet. I'll get the pillows from the lawn chairs."

"You girls all right?" Mary inquired from the kitchen.

"Yes, Mom. We're waiting for the Niffits."

Dex and Roxy sat waiting for about ten minutes, barely speaking, checking their watches and occasionally looking at each other. They both laughed.

Roxy said, "I feel kind of foolish sitting here waiting for some little green people. What would we tell people if they found out what we're doing?"

"Well, I'd say we were just inspecting the grass." Dexie giggled.

"Yeah and asking it questions." Roxy also giggled.

Dexie glanced at Roxie, "Do you think they're coming, Rox?"

"Oh, I hope so. Let's be really quiet so we don't scare them."

Both girls heard a tapping from the karaoke player and looked at the black plastic box sitting on the ground. Akira was striking the karaoke machine with a little twig and Masako was standing near him looking up at the two female giants.

Simultaneously, the girls said, "There they are!"

Roxy spoke softly, "Good morning. We were afraid you wouldn't come. We want you to talk into this so we can hear you better." Roxy placed the microphone on the ground a few inches from the Niffits. When she moved the microphone toward the little people, the Niffits grabbed each other and cowered down against the black plastic box.

"Oh! I'm sorry I scared you. Let me show you what this is for."

Roxy picked up the mic and talked into it, her voice amplified by the karaoke amplifier.

Dexie looked out from behind the camcorder and responded with, "See, it makes your voices louder so we can hear what you say."

The Niffits stepped forward and bowed to the girls.

"They understand, Roxy!"

Roxy placed the mic next to the Niffits and they stepped closer to it. Masako reached out and tapped on the microphone. The little niffit smiled when she heard the thumps from the amplifier.

Roxy and Dex heard "Ohayougozaimasu—Good morning," from Akira, followed by *"morning,"* from Masako.

Roxy looked at Dex and grinned, then said, "Dex, you go first."

Dexie spoke calmly and quietly, "How did you live on the big water?"

Akira said, "Big wood, broken building, broken building. Big ship pull building from water, from water. Hide on ship until it stop, until it stop. Get in box, in box."

Akira looked at Masako, waved his hands, spoke to her and she said, "truck?"

"Ahso! Truck takes big box on road, on road. We tired, so get off, get off."

Roxy asked, "How did you learn English?"

"We listen to TV, TV," Akira replied, looked at Masako, then the girls, and the two Niffits grinned, proud of their accomplishment.

Roxy and Dex talked with the Niffits for several minutes before showing the little people the dollhouse. Roxy got the play house from the garage and set it next to the microphone.

The Niffits were very curious and cautiously began to investigate the miniature building.

In less than a minute Akira returned to the microphone and asked, "For us?"

"Yes, if you like. We will fix it so you will be warm when it gets very cold."

"We stay warm, stay warm," the Niffits replied. "We show, show."

Akira and Masako faced each other, held hands, touched stomachs together, hummed and their bodies began to glow light green like small fluorescent bulbs.

They glowed for about five seconds, stepped back from each other and the radiance vanished.

Akira said, "Star bugs, star bugs, but warm, warm." Both Niffits smiled.

Dexie said, "I think they mean fireflies, Rox."

The Niffits looked at each other and whispered. Akira poked Masako so she would speak into the microphone.

"We go home soon?"

Roxy paused and answered, "We don't have the money to go to Japan right now. We are working on a way to take you back home."

Akira and Masako listened intently and bowed when they understood.

Akira asked, "Can send in box, in box?"

Roxy quickly answered, "No. In an airplane, a box would have no air to breathe and would be very cold." She suddenly remembered the clothes Dexie had made. "We have something for you." Roxy pointed at the box of clothes so Dexie would bring the container close to the microphone. "Show them, Dexie."

Dexie reached behind her and picked up the small box, opened it and put the tiny clothes on the grass in front of the Niffits.

"I made you these for your trip to Japan, but you can use them any time. I hope you like them," Dex smiled.

The Niffits touched the tiny outfits and Masako said, "Oh, soft." Akira pulled on a tiny blue shirt and rubbed the cloth with his hands.

Akira said, "Me like." "Me like," Masako echoed.

The Niffits said, "Domo-arigato, domo-arigato—Thank you," and bowed to each of the girls.

"You are welcome," Dex replied.

"My father will fix the house for you, but we have to move it to the backyard so it can't be seen from the street. I'm worried about cats and dogs attacking you." Roxy was really worried.

"You need not worry," Akira advised, "animals do not like our smell."

Dexie clapped her hands, laughed, and said, "Little green skunks!"

Roxy added, "We'll figure out a way to get you home. When we are ready to talk again, in the afternoon, we'll leave a coin like this, in the grass where we are now." Roxy held up a nickel. "We'll talk the next day, in the afternoon. Is that all right?"

Akira nodded and said, "Yes. Masako and I will watch for the disk." The Niffits ran off into the grass.

The girls left the box of little clothes on the ground, stood, and picked up the equipment. Rox and Dex put the karaoke amplifier and camcorder in the garage and returned to retrieve the box. All the tiny clothes were gone, but at the bottom of the box was a shiny new penny.

Rox and Dex both had tears in their eyes. They looked at each other and hugged. The connection with the little Niffits had been a resounding success.

"We have to get them back to Japan, Dex."

Dex replied, "When our parents get together with us tonight, do you think we can figure it out?"

"Oh, I sure hope so!"

Chapter 13

Surprising News

Rox and Dex spent the rest of the day surfing the Web looking for the cheapest expense for three to Japan. They found a church group planning a trip during the second week in December, but it was limited to Seventh Day Adventists, and the girls and Mrs. Maxwell didn't qualify. An hour of work at the computer resulted in tired eyes and disappointment. Dex returned home and Roxy went to her room and took a nap.

In the afternoon, the girls went to a mall with their mothers and purchased some winter clothes. While walking the mall, Karen Chappell and Mary found time to talk about the Niffits. Dex's mom was shocked to find out from Mary that the Niffits really existed. She had thought the girls were just making up a fanciful story about little green people from Japan. Mrs. Chappell was anxious to see the camcorder video and expected the Maxwell family to come over to visit around 7:30 p.m.

Roxy and her mom cleaned up after dinner. Loading the dishwasher was Roxy's job and Mary stored the leftovers in Tupperware and placed the containers in the refrigerator. Carl watched the network TV news and began viewing a university soccer match on one of the sports channels. It seemed like only a few minutes had elapsed since dinner and it was 7:15, time to walk to the Chappells' for the two-family conference. Roxy picked up the camcorder, locked the front door and joined her parents for the walk down the street.

The two-tone doorbell announced their arrival at Chappells'. Dex had been waiting at the door watching the Maxwells approach, opened it and invited the visitors into the living room.

Bruce was sitting in an overstuffed chair reading the financial section of last Sunday's newspaper. Karen came out of the kitchen, Bruce stood and the adults all shook hands.

"Have a seat, folks," Bruce offered the sofa with a sweep of his arm. "I'm very curious to see this video of the—the Niffits?"

Carl asked, "How should we do this girls? Roxy, why don't you sit on the sofa and hold the camcorder with your mom and dad on either side. We'll stand up behind the sofa and watch. Okay? Dexie, stand between me and your mom."

Everyone got rearranged and Roxy looked up at the Chappells. She started the recording and turned up the volume. As the video replayed, Karen and Bruce could not believe what they saw, but they settled down and concentrated on the activities and words of the Niffits. When the last of the conversations with the Niffits terminated, the Chappells sat stunned. Karen and Bruce looked at each other and then at the Maxwells, unable to say anything.

Bruce was first to speak, "Well I'll be darned."

"I still don't believe it, but they sure are cute little beings, aren't they?" responded Mary. She had seen the video before but it still was hard for her to accept the reality of the little people from Japan.

Roxy and Dex took turns telling Mary and Bruce Chappell the details of how they wanted to take the Niffits back to Japan, but the cost of the plane tickets was prohibitive.

"How much is a ticket, Dex?" her father asked.

Dex glanced at Roxy and said, "A round trip ticket is about sixteen hundred dollars for one person." Dex looked at her dad, her face expressing the disappointment.

Mr. Chappell thought for a moment and said, "I just had an idea." He paused for a moment. "You know, it just might work!"

Everyone looked at Bruce, waiting for him to explain, but instead, he asked a question.

"Girls, what is four times sixteen hundred?"

A short silent pause occurred. Roxy and Dex simultaneously answered, "Sixty-four hundred. Why?"

"Well, the head office of the bank has a planned trip to Greece for the top twenty branch managers and their families, but I can't go. Karen has some charity work to do, so she can't go. But I think I can get the tickets changed to another place since we have already been to Greece."

Karen said, "But Bruce, we haven't been to Greece!"

"That's true, but we don't want to go to Greece, we want to go to Japan," he smiled. "As long as the money is used for a vacation, the bank doesn't really care where we go. They apparently received a group rate for the trip to Greece. One family, more or less, won't make any difference."

Dex said, "So who is going to Japan, Dad? You and Mom, Roxy and me?"

"No, Dex. Roxy, you and Mr. and Mrs. Maxwell will go. What about it, Maxwells?"

Mary looked at Carl questioningly and answered, "That would be wonderful! But Carl, can you get away from work?"

"Oh yeah! For a trip to Japan—definitely! We have a little money in reserve so we could stay for maybe—" He looked at Mary, "a week?"

Bruce said, "Dex, would you please get me my briefcase?"

"Sure, Dad." Dex jumped up from the sofa, turned to Roxy, smiled and gave her a high five.

Dex picked up her father's briefcase, which was on the floor next to the front door and carried it to her dad. Bruce opened a white plastic folder and pulled a sheet of paper from the inside pocket and began quickly reading through a two-page letter, each page exhibiting the bank's red and blue logo.

"Ah, here it is." He read aloud, "Each family will be allocated a maximum of eight thousand dollars and may take guests on their trip."

He put the papers back in his briefcase and said, "You have eight thousand dollars, Maxwells! I will have to sign for the tickets, so send me the information and I will obtain the tickets for you. You have until December 30 to take the trip."

Dex and Roxy had gone into the kitchen and gotten some ice cream and were sitting at the table talking excitedly about taking the Niffits back to Japan. They had to plan and carry out every movement perfectly to get the Niffits successfully past the scrutiny of the TSA guards.

In the living room, the adults were discussing the details for booking the flight and accommodations for the stay in Japan. Maxwells had agreed to leave for Japan on December 20, on Wednesday. They just had to pay some bills, put a hold on their mail and get their clothes ready. The girls were to get the Niffits ready for the flight. They thought they had plenty of time.

Chapter 14

Weighing In

Following the round of thanks to Bruce Chappell for the opportunity to take the Niffits to Japan and, in addition, have a vacation, Maxwells said goodnight and began walking home. They had just crossed the street when Dex came running from her house.

"Roxy! Don't forget to put a nickel out so we can talk to the Niffits after school."

"Okay, Dex. Thanks for reminding me. See you in the morning!"

Roxy and Dex waved to each other and Dex disappeared into her house.

As they continued walking, Mary said, "That was sure nice of Bruce to offer us the use of his vacation tickets, wasn't it?"

Carl replied, "Yeah. I've always thought he was a stuffed shirt. He has never asked me to play golf with him."

"Honey, you don't even know how to play golf," Mary laughed.

"I know, but it's the thought that counts," Carl grinned.

Roxy added, "When Dex and I were in the kitchen, she said she was shocked that her dad came up with the idea of providing the money for the tickets. She has new respect for her dad now. Dex told me her dad must have had a good week at the bank or her mom told him he didn't have to take her dancing at the club."

Mary looked at her daughter and said, "Dexie told you that?"

"Uh-huh. She told me her dad doesn't like to dance. He feels like a dope."

As the Maxwells entered their driveway, Roxy pulled on her dad's shirtsleeve and asked, "Brother, can you spare a dime?" and laughed.

"Where did you get that, Roxy?" quizzed her mom. "That was in a song from the Great Depression."

"School!" Roxy answered with an ear-to-ear grin. "Sometimes I come up with some good ones, huh?"

"Here you go, smarty pants." Grinning, Carl fished a dime from his pocket flipped it to Roxy.

Roxy caught the coin, dropped into her pocket, pulled out a nickel and placed it in the grass for the Niffits to find and know to meet the girls in the afternoon.

"I thought you wanted a dime for that, Roxy."

"Half-off on Sunday, Dad!" She laughed as they went in the house.

Roxy finally went to sleep early Monday morning. She had crawled between the sheets around ten o'clock but just couldn't stop thinking about the procedure the girls and the Niffits would have to follow to get the little visitors on a plane without being noticed. Every time she thought of the possibility of someone detecting the Niffits, she got the shivers. If they were caught with the little people, she kept thinking, "Will the FBI wring the truth out of me. Could I stand up to truth serum? Would I confess?

Roxy was taken to a room and left alone for an hour. Two large men carrying folders entered and sat down across from her at a big metal table. Suddenly, a buzzer went off and one of the men reached for his cell phone. He was talking on the phone, but it kept ringing."

"Roxy! Your alarm! Time to get up and get ready for school."

It was her mom's voice that brought her out of the dream and back to reality. Roxy sat up, reached over and turned the alarm off. The time was 6:47. The alarm had been buzzing for two minutes. Roxy stretched and yawned and suddenly realized she had to get ready for riding the bus and talking with Dean. He would want to know what the plans were for taking the Niffits home to Japan. She slipped into her new jeans and a sweatshirt and ran down to the kitchen.

Mary had gotten some juice and cereal ready. She had sliced half a banana into disks on top of the cereal. Roxy added some milk, sat down, and shoveled it in her mouth. The spoon wasn't doing a good job so she pushed in some of the cereal with her fingers—and got the hiccups.

"Drink some milk, dear, and then your orange juice. That should take care of the hiccups."

Roxy heard knocking at the back door and Dex's head appeared, looking through the glass panes into the kitchen. Roxy opened the door and said, "Hi Dex, are you ready?"

Dex yawned, blinked her eyes and said, "I couldn't go to sleep last night. I kept thinking of going to Japan and taking the Niffits back home."

Roxy replied, "I had a bad dream, but I don't remember what is was about except it had something to do with the FBI. Why are you here? We usually meet at the bus stop."

Dexie shrugged her shoulders and said, "I didn't want to wait for you at the bus stop." She tilted her head and looked behind Roxy.

"Hi Mrs. Maxwell!"

"Hi Dexie! Have a good day at school, girls."

Roxy and Dexie didn't talk with Dean until after school. He was sitting with another boy on the bus to school, so they didn't talk in the morning. When they got off the bus after school, Dean asked about the Sunday meeting with the Niffits. They filled him in on the plans to go to Japan.

Dexie said, "We can't take you with us, Dean, but you will be very important to the success of the mission."

"What's that?"

"You will have to toss the model plane to us to get the Niffits past the magnetic scanner and the x-ray machine."

"Oh, yeah. I can do that, but we'll have to practice a lot to make sure it works."

Roxy nodded, "Exactly. I think you can do it."

The girls plugged in the karaoke machine, checked the camcorder and set up their equipment on the driveway next to the corner of the house where Roxy had dropped the nickel the night before. The coin was on the concrete. The two pixies appeared about ten minutes later. They were dressed in some of the clothes Dex had presented to them, looking like little dolls. After saying hello and bowing to the girls, Akira and Masako sat down in the grass next to the microphone and waited for the girls to speak. They were watching Dean closely.

"We have good news for you. We are going to take you to Japan in December, about eighty days from now. Dexie and I will have to practice getting you through the inspection area so no one sees you. A little airplane will carry you over the equipment that might hurt or discover you. We'll do some test flights out here in the grass first. You will have to come in our house so we can try our ideas without the outside wind and grass causing problems, too. Can you do that?"

The Niffits turned to each other and jabbered back and forth for a few seconds.

Akira looked up at the girls and spoke into the microphone, "We can do." Masako gave her usual echo. Akira asked, "When? When?"

Roxy suddenly realized by the way they were reacting, the Niffits seemed to have some urgency about getting back to Japan. "Akira, are you and Masako in a hurry to go to Japan?"

Akira stepped closer to the microphone and replied, "We are expecting a miffit before long."

Roxy and Dexie had never heard miffit before, but when Akira said 'expecting' they realized a miffit was a baby niffit. It would be born before long.

Dexie spoke first. "Oh. When will the little one arrive?"

Akira said, "When six blossoms come." He held up six fingers.

"Yes—six." Masako smiled. "We must be home for its arrival. Mother must help."

Roxy and Dexie didn't get it. "What do you mean by six blossoms?" Roxy inquired.

Masako pointed at the blossom at the top of her head. "Another comes soon."

Roxy did a quick calculation. "Dex, that means another blossom every three weeks."

Masako whispered to Akira and pointed at Dean.

"Who is brown boy?" Akira pointed at Dean.

Roxy was embarrassed. "Oh, I'm sorry. That is our friend, Dean. He will help with the airplane."

The Niffits bowed toward Dean and he said, "Happy to meet you people, Mr. and Mrs. Niffit."

Akira and Masako smiled and Akira responded, almost indignantly, "We not people; we Niffits."

Dean, being very curious, had to ask, "What is your last name?"

Akira frowned and said, "Only one name each." He pointed at his wife and said, "Masako," and thrust his left index finger in his chest and said, "Akira."

Dexie giggled and looked at Dean. "I guess he told you, but that was a good question, Dean."

As Roxy's smile faded, she got back to business. She leaned toward the Niffits and said, "We have to find how much you weigh. Dex, could you ask my mom for the postal scale?"

Dexie went to the back door, knocked, and spoke through the screen door. She asked Mary for the scale used for weighing letters to determine postage and returned in less than a minute. Roxy put her hand, palm up, on the ground and asked the Niffits to climb on, which they did, but a little hesitantly. She moved her hand containing the Niffits next to the platform on top of the scale and said, "Akira and Masako, please get onto the metal platform so we can weigh you."

As the Niffits hopped from Roxy's palm to the scale, Roxy laughed and scratched her palm with her fingers.

"They tickle!"

Dex read the blue LED and said, "They weigh 3.3 ounces. Now have Masako get off so we can see what Akira weighs, then we'll have both weights."

Masako had heard what Dex said and jumped off the scale onto Roxy's extended open hand. The LED read 1.8 ounces.

"So, Masako weighs 1.5 ounces," Dex commented.

"Okay, now we can balance the weight on the airplane so it flies straight. We'll use pennies to balance the weight. Let's see what some pennies weigh. Dex, do you have some pennies with you?"

Dex checked her pockets and said, "Nope. You get some and I'll put Akira back on the ground with Masako."

Roxy ran in the house and came back with a roll of pennies. She broke open the paper roll and poured a bunch of pennies on the concrete. The Niffits reacted excitedly, never having seen so many pennies at one time. They pointed at the coins and jabbered back and forth. Roxy counted out the pennies as she placed them on the postal scale. One ounce was equivalent to ten pennies. They could balance Akira's weight with Masako and three pennies.

Roxy said, "I guess the Niffits can go for now. We will have to make paper airplanes that can carry the 3.6-ounce weight and still glide. What do you think, Dex?"

"I think you're right. I'll tell the Niffits they can go now but return tomorrow, same time. We'll put a nickel out tonight to make sure they come back."

"Sounds like a plan, Dex."

Chapter 15

Test Flights

Roxy stuck her pennies in her pocket and the girls put away the equipment. They had to design a paper airplane that could carry the weight of the Niffits. Dean had told them a regular paper plane made from notebook paper wouldn't work; it would be too flimsy. He suggested wood or cardboard as other alternatives. The plane had to carry the Niffits and three pennies, a total of 3.6 ounces.

The team went to Roxy's bedroom and sat on the bed thinking how to make a simple airplane that would carry the precious cargo. The plane would have to glide about ten feet and land gently so Akira and Masako wouldn't be injured.

Dex said, "Could we use construction paper?"

"I'm telling you, that won't work. We need something stronger than paper." Dean was sure paper wouldn't work.

Roxy glanced at Dexie and said, "Well, let's try some cardboard. I've got some pieces in my hobby desk drawer."

"Okay. I'll make the wings, you can make the body, Rox."

"Dean, you make the tail section."

"Okay, the rudder and the stabilizer—coming up!"

"Dex, the body is called the fuselage," Roxy smiled.

"Jeez, Rox! Don't get technical on me," Dex laughed.

Five minutes later, the wings were attached with Magic tape and the model was tested with a 2.0 ounce weight, about half of what they needed. The model was better than the paper airplanes but still not right, lacking control, the plane nosedived to the floor.

"Hey, you three, time for a snack!" Roxy's mom called from the bottom of the stairs.

While they ate, Roxy, Dean, and Dex discussed the trial and error approach they would use. Mary could not help the team but made a good suggestion.

"Roxy, why don't you ask your dad for some help? He'll be home for dinner before long."

The team was still at the table talking when Carl arrived home a little early for dinner. In preparation for the flight to Japan, he had been tying up loose ends at work getting some city projects scheduled for the time he was to be out of the country.

"Dad! We need your help," was the first thing Carl heard when he opened the front door and stepped into the living room. He made his way into the kitchen and sat down at the table with the three airplane-designers.

"What can I help you with?" Carl asked as Mary handed him a cookie on a saucer and a mug of steaming-hot black coffee.

Each team member expressed thoughts about constructing a glider that could carry the weight of two Niffits. As Carl nibbled his cookie, he listened intently to what the team related. A few moments after the girls and Dean finished their proposals, Carl washed down the last morsel with a sip from his mug and said, "Okay, I have an idea for you to try. I think it will work."

"We have a big, corrugated cardboard box that the clothes dryer came in. It's folded up and stored above the ceiling in the garage. I'll get it for you after I have another cookie. Okay?" Carl looked at his wife questioningly, expecting her to say it would be better to eat an apple, but he thought he'd make the attempt for another cookie.

As the cookie disappeared, they talked about the upcoming trip to Japan and the plan to get the Niffits on the plane. Carl took a small notebook from his shirt pocket and started sketching right after he mentioned the box in the garage.

"Okay, here's your passenger plane."

Carl tore out a page from his notebook and turned it so the kids could see what he had drawn. The girls looked at the sketch and then at each other and smiled. Dean had no comment.

"Awesome, Dad! But what is that thing in the middle of the fuselage?"

"Well, that's the passenger compartment. It's made from a toilet tissue tube with one end closed off so the Niffits won't fall out."

"Can we make it, Dad? How big is it? How do you know it will fly?"

"So many questions! Oh, it will fly. I made gliders from balsa wood when I was your age. All my airplanes were great gliders. I'll get the box from the garage."

Carl pushed his chair back, went out the kitchen door to the garage and returned in less than a minute with a large folded up Maytag box.

"Get a ruler, Rox, and some tape. I'll get a utility knife and a marker and you will have your airplane constructed before dinner."

The girls measured the sketch, as Dean watched, anticipating errors. Carl had expanded the sketch on the cardboard, making it four times larger. Using the utility knife, Carl cut out the pieces and they assembled the glider. Roxy scoured the two bathroom cabinets but couldn't find a toilet paper cylinder. But Mary retrieved a cylinder from a roll of paper towels. After cutting the tube to size, they taped one end shut and installed it in the fuselage.

"Is it ready, Mr. Maxwell?"

"Almost, Dex. We need to put thirty-six pennies in a plastic sandwich bag and put it in the passenger compartment. We have to simulate the weight of the Niffits plus the ballast to balance the airplane so it will glide just right. We'll probably have to make a few adjustments. Let's take the plane outside and give it a try."

Roxy stacked the pennies in a small plastic bag, taped it to maintain the cylindrical shape, and stuffed the bag into the cylinder located in the center of the fuselage. Since Dean was going to launch the Niffits' airplane at the airport, he would make all the test throws. His experience with the glider might be the difference between success and failure.

Out in the backyard, the girls paced off about twenty feet, turned and faced Dean, nothing but grass between them. Dean would toss the plane and Roxy or Dexie would attempt to catch it.

"Okay, here it comes!" Dean announced.

The plane glided through the air and landed at Roxy's feet. Roxy had to jump back so the glider wouldn't hit her. She wasn't able to even try to catch the plane.

"Okay girls, some small adjustments are necessary."

Carl slid the wing about a half-inch toward the nose of the aircraft, taped it in place and handed the glider back to Dean.

"Dean, when you toss the plane, launch it with a little more oomph."

Dex and Roxy broke out laughing, having never heard the word oomph before.

Carl laughed and said, "Oomph means throw the plane a little harder but still have it under control."

This time, Dean's toss was perfect and the plane sailed right into Roxy's hands about waist high.

"Now you've got it! Practice so you can do it perfectly ten times in a row. Then we'll add some difficulty. Come and get me when you're ready. I'm going in to talk to Mary."

About ten minutes elapsed before Roxy called for her dad. They tried a couple more practice tosses before Carl returned to the backyard. But he didn't stop; he walked past the young people into the garage and came back with a broom, a rake, and a fold-up yard chair.

"What are you doing, Dad?"

"I'm putting some people and a chair in your way so you will have some obstacles for the plane to avoid."

Carl got several bricks and inserted the handles of the broom and rake in the holes in the large bricks so the tools would simulate people being in the way at the airport. He placed the chair in front of Roxy so she would have to reach over it to catch the glider.

"Try it now. This should be a little more difficult, but with practice, you should still be able to toss and catch the plane. If you have some crashes, we can fix the plane, so don't worry about that."

Carl went back into the kitchen, sat down with another cup of coffee. Mary and Carl talked about the upcoming trip to Japan. They could hear the frustration in the girls' voices turn to jubilation after ten minutes of practice with the glider. Carl went to the window above the sink and watched the girls as Dean tossed the plane several more times. He looked at his watch and decided to watch TV until dinner was ready. He stopped at the kitchen counter, gave Mary a kiss on the forehead and said, "Tell the aeronautical engineers that I'll be available for consultation until dinner time. Let me know if you need any assistance. I can mash potatoes, you know."

"Okay, dear. Go watch TV or take a nap. Dinner is a half-hour away."

Before the flight team separated for the evening, they decided to simulate the airplane tosses every few days as long as the weather was nice. They wanted to maintain their readiness for the actual event. They only talked with the Niffits once a week, but they began to notice Masako gaining weight, and the blossoms were accumulating.

The first week in November arrived quickly. Masako's flower had three blossoms and her tummy was noticeably enlarging, but still only a medium-sized bump. Dean commented that when she looked like she had swallowed a whole grape, it would be about time for her baby to arrive.

Chapter 16

Final Preparation

The three-person crew practiced with the airplane until they were more than ninety-five percent successful. The girls moved the broom, rake, and chair into different configurations and maintained their high percentage of safe catches. Dean had adjusted his tossing slightly after having only made a single bad throw. One night during Thanksgiving break from school after practicing the toss and catch routine, they sat down in the grass and reviewed the operation to get the Niffits past the screeners.

Dex said, "I'll put a message in the compartment that says good-bye and have a nice trip. If the TSA people take the plane, they'll find the note."

Roxy commented, "I'll have to conceal the Niffits. I might have to fall down so they can hide in my pocket after they get out of the glider. Then they can get in Mom's purse. We'll take the Niffit dolls in that little box with their clothes. Also, we'll need some food for them and maybe some toilet tissue."

The girls laughed, thinking about the Niffits needing a bathroom.

"What do you think they eat, Dean?"

"Gosh, I don't know. We'd better ask them. Let's put a nickel out in the grass so they'll come tomorrow. We need to practice with them and find the answers to our questions. Let's tell them if you don't catch the glider, they'll need to hide in your mom's purse until we're all on the plane."

The Niffits were waiting when the girls set up the equipment. The sun was out, but it was typical November weather and cool. The nighttime temperatures were dropping to the low forties. Akira and Masako were dressed in clothes Dexie had made. Akira wore a hat but Masako didn't try to cover her blossoms, which now numbered four.

Following the exchange of greetings, Dex and Roxy explained the procedures for getting on the jet to Japan. Then, Dex said, "What do you like to eat?"

Akira answered, "Nibbles and bites are very good, very good."

Dex looked at Roxy and frowned. Dean said, "Oh, I know! Kibbles n' Bits. You know, the dog food."

Dex broke out laughing, "Where have they been eating, a dog kennel?"

Akira said, "We find food where dogs are staying, are staying."

Dexie asked, "Do you like that food?"

"It is okay, but not Japanese food." Masako looked at Akira for approval. He nodded his acceptance of her comment.

Dean volunteered, "Would they like some Thanksgiving food? We always have leftovers at our house."

Akira spoke up, "We think Kibbles okay, not change now before travel."

Roxy replied, "Okay, we'll make sure we have some for you and we'll get some water on the airplane. Now, we need to have you fly in our airplane."

Dean held the glider and Roxy had the Niffits get on the palm of her right hand. Making sure they didn't fall off, she raised her hand to the glider, pointed with her left forefinger and whispered, "Please get in the little airplane where that hole is. Masako should be on the side with the coins."

Akira nodded his tiny head and climbed on one side of the open cylinder. He reached up and helped Masako slide in beside him. They waved to the girls.

"I guess we're ready, Dean. We'll get into position and you can launch the glider."

Roxy and Dexie assumed their usual positions and said, "Okay, Dean, send the Niffits on their maiden flight."

Dean took a deep breath, raised the glider above his head and tossed it.

Roxy didn't move an inch and caught the glider easily. The little plane flew straight as an arrow between the broom and the rake into her outstretched hands. She looked into the compartment to see Akira and Masako waving to her. The maiden flight was successful!

"Good throw, Dean. The passengers are fine. Let's do it again. This time Dexie will catch it."

After two successful trials, Dexie said, "I think it's gliding a little lower than before. Could the weight of the miffit make a difference?"

"Yeah. I'll take out one penny, we only need two."

Roxy had the Niffits climb out and Dean removed one of the three ballast coins. The Niffits slid back into the passenger compartment.

"We're not going to catch it this time so don't throw it too high, Dean. We'll let it glide to the ground."

Dex told the Niffits what they were going to do and told them to hang on tightly.

The plane glided through the obstacles, caught a wing tip in the grass and flipped over. The girls ran to the plane and carefully righted the glider, looking into the compartment. Akira and Masako hadn't fallen out but were a little shaken by the experience. Dex held the plane and the Niffits crawled out onto Roxy's hand. The girls went over to the karaoke equipment and put the little people next to the microphone.

Akira spoke into the microphone, "We little bit scared but okay, okay."

"We are sorry the plane crashed, but that might really happen at the airport. If something happens so I can't pick you up, you need to get into my mother's purse. Just a minute and I will show you the purse."

Roxy stood up and ran in the house, the screen door banging behind her. A minute later, she brought back her mother's black purse and placed it on the ground beside the Niffits.

"This is the purse my mother will have at the airport. She will put it on the floor next to her. You will have to hide in it until we get on the big airplane. I will try to help you, but if I can't, you will have to climb in the purse by yourselves. If someone sees you or touches you, play dead so they will think you are dolls. Dex and I will rescue you if we get separated. The trip will be a long one and many people will be sleeping. That will be the time to move around in the airplane. Do you have any questions?"

Akira answered, "Not now, thank you. Maybe tomorrow, after we think, we think."

"Okay. Tomorrow, we'll practice again and you can ask us questions."

The Niffits bowed to the girls, Masako waved and the little people ran toward their home.

"I just remembered, Rox, we need to paint the glider green. Does your dad have any green spray paint?"

"There's some painting stuff in the garage. Let's put the karaoke equipment away and look for paint. If we find some green paint and it's not in a spray can, we can use some of your watercolor brushes, Dex."

"Yeah, I've got some old brushes that will work. It should only take a few minutes to make the fuselage green. We can always get some green paint at the craft store if we can't find any in the garage."

The girls found a small can of light green paint and a couple of one-inch brushes in a cabinet. Roxy spread a newspaper on the garage floor and the girls began to paint the wing. Dean found another small brush and painted the fuselage and tail section. In about ten minutes, the entire plane was green.

Just as they finished painting, Roxy inspected their work and said, "I kind of like the color."

Smiling, Dexie observed, "Perfect, you guys—niffit green!"

After cleaning the brushes, it occurred to Roxy the weight of the paint might have changed the flight characteristics of the glider.

"Dean, we've made the plane a little heavier by painting the whole thing. Maybe we should have just painted the fuselage? What do you think?"

Dean picked up the airplane but quickly put it back on the newspapers, thinking the paint was wet and looked at his hands.

"Hey! It's dry! Let's do another test flight."

Dean launched the plane toward Roxy but the glider sailed over Roxy's head, made a loop, and crashed into a tree. Roxy ran to the plane and inspected it. No damage was found and she handed the glider to Dean.

Roxy looked at Dex and said, "We screwed up; we forgot the weight of the Niffits!"

"Oh, gosh, you're right! Get the pennies and we'll try it again."

Dean held the plane while Roxy slid the pennies into the cargo compartment.

"Okay! Get ready to catch it, Rox."

Dean tossed the loaded glider but it didn't glide as far as it had previously, so Roxy moved the wing slightly forward, and Dean gave the glider a second toss. The plane flew perfectly across the yard and into Dexie's outstretched arms.

"Awesome, Rox. We're ready for the Niffits to take their last test flight for November."

The test flight was completed successfully and the Niffits were told to be ready to go to Japan in three weeks. The Niffits said they were scared but they had no questions. The team would continue the practice flights substituting pennies for the Niffits. There was no reason to risk injuring the little beings, especially Masako.

Chapter 17

Boarding the Plane

The second week in December was the beginning of active preparation for the trip to Japan. The girls found a nickel by the steps and the next day the Niffits appeared after school. Five blossoms were present on Masako's pretty little head, signaling the upcoming birth. When the sixth blossom appeared, the birth was about to occur; the Niffits had to be back in Japan.

After a brief conversation with the Niffits, Roxy called Dean and asked him to come over. When Dean arrived he had bad news, he just found out he couldn't go to the airport the day the Niffits were to leave for their home country. His parents had left him a note to read when he got home from school.

"But why won't your parents let you go to the airport, Dean?" Dexie was a little frustrated with the late development.

"Dad said I couldn't go, but I couldn't explain why I wanted to—because it was a secret. I couldn't break my word to you guys." Dean hung his head and a tear fell to the kitchen floor.

Mary had been listening from the living room and came into the kitchen. "Here, Dean, have a cookie, I made two dozen more." She handed Dean a cookie and said, "Let's take the camcorder over to your house and show your mom the recording of the Niffits."

"You, you'd do that?"

Dexie stated, "Sure, Dean, you're part of the team—a very important part."

"When will your mom be home today?" Roxy asked.

Dean perked up, "About four o'clock."

Mary glanced at the clock, "We've got fifteen minutes. Girls, get the recorder ready. We'll take a little walk." Mary gave Dean another cookie and retrieved her heavy sweater from the bedroom. The girls disappeared upstairs to get the camcorder. Dean was feeling better, knowing Mrs. Maxwell and the girls would convince his mom she should let him take part in the plan to get the Niffits home before the sixth blossom appeared.

Mrs. Walker, Cynthia, was surprised to find her son, two girls, and Mrs. Maxwell sitting on her front porch when she pulled into the driveway. She got out of the car with some groceries and said, "Mrs. Maxwell, what can I do for you?"

Mary smiled and replied, "Something very important, Cynthia. We want you to see something your son has been participating in since the beginning of October."

"Well, all right. Let's all go inside."

Following the recording, and the oral reports from the team, Cynthia sat quietly for a moment. "I don't know what I'm going to tell my husband, but I'll take Dean to the airport. Please give me the details and we'll be there."

Dean threw his arms around his mom and said, "Thank you, thank you, thank you."

Cynthia was a little emotional, her eyes began to water. "I didn't know how important you were to the plan to get the Niffits back home. I thought you were just going to do something crazy."

When they had time, the girls' mothers spent the remaining days shopping for clothes for the trip to Japan. Just when they thought every possibility was covered, they had to go get something else. The night before takeoff, Dex stayed overnight at Maxwells' so everything was coordinated the morning of the flight.

Even though every possible contingency had been thought of and planned for, everyone was a little nervous the morning of the flight. The Maxwells, Dexie and the Niffits went to the airport two hours before takeoff to meet with Dean and his mom before preparation for boarding occurred. Dean's mom would have the Niffits and Dean had the airplane. Cynthia followed the Maxwells' car and would park and wait for a call from Mary.

Cynthia had the Niffits in her pocket. They would be transferred to the glider at the last minute. The glider's passenger section was going to be a tight fit for the two little people, both wearing some of the clothes Dex had made. Masako's tummy bulge made for a tight fit in the compartment. Dean stayed outside the terminal with his mom but was able to watch Maxwells pass through the screening process and take seats in the boarding area, which wasn't the same distance as all their plans had assumed; it was almost twice as far away from the ticket counter, roped off from the boarding area.

Roxy walked around nervously, looking out at the big passenger jet and then back toward the screening area. Her mom and dad sat in metal-framed chairs, as did several other passengers. A few people stood at the big windows watching the activity on the tarmac. It looked like about twenty-five to thirty people would be getting on board the plane to join the passengers already on the jet.

At the last minute, Dean said, "Mom! I forgot the note to Roxy and Dexie that I was supposed to put in the glider! How stupid of me!"

"Don't worry, Dean, I've got some paper and we can write with my lipstick."

"Oh, thanks, Mom. You are a lifesaver! I could have ruined our whole plan!"

Dean printed the words as quickly as he could, hastily put the note in the compartment and ran back to his position. He looked through the big windows to see what the departure time was, observing it change from 30 to 15 minutes. Time for action!

Dean held the plane as Cynthia helped the Niffits get into position. Then Dean went into the terminal, sat down next to a newspaper stand and tried to look relaxed. He looked down at the Niffits and whispered, "Are you ready?"

Akira waved to Dean, indicating he and Masako were prepared. Dean began walking toward the roped off area about thirty-five- to forty-feet from Roxy. When he reached the rope, he raised the plane over his head and yelled, "Roxy!"

Roxy stood up on the seat she had taken next to her mother, turned toward Dean and located him. He seemed so far away! Dean had realized the glider was going to travel much farther than they had planned, so he hopped on top of a book stand for greater elevation and tossed the glider with some extra oomph. The little plane with its precious cargo flew straight as an arrow toward Roxy who

was readying herself to catch the glider. About five feet from the target, a lady suddenly stood up and the airplane hit the woman in the head, glanced off and crashed about ten feet from Roxy. But Dexie was running toward the stricken plane.

Pandemonium broke out. Whistles sounded and TSA people came from all directions, two of them jumped over the ropes and headed for Roxy. Two other guards were moving toward the glider, but Roxy beat them to it. She huddled over it and helped the Niffits get from the compartment onto the floor. Roxy needed a distraction, so she pretended to trip over one of the waiting area chairs as she got up from the floor. That diversion was all the Niffits needed. They scrambled under the chairs and climbed into a black purse.

Dean was watching intently. Suddenly, he felt a hand grabbing him around the neck and another hand was squeezing his throwing arm. A big man with a potbelly had latched onto him. He was able to see Roxy being corralled by two women, one of which had the glider in her hands. Mrs. Maxwell was talking on her cell phone.

A gruff male voice said, "You're coming with me young man!"

Dean relaxed and the fingers around his neck were loosened a bit, but he had no intention of trying to get away. The plan looked like it was working. The agents took Roxy and Dean to a room and sat them down opposite two uniformed agents, a man and a woman, seated at a large, cold, metal table.

The woman, who must have been a supervisor, because she wore a different uniform than the other agents and seemed to be in charge asked Dean, "What was that all about, throwing something that hadn't passed through security to your friend. I assume this young lady is your friend?"

"Yes, ma'am. I just wanted to wish her a safe trip because I missed the girls when they left the neighborhood this morning. I wrote a note and put it in the airplane. You can check and see."

The TSA woman holding the glider looked at the little airplane.

Dean said, "Look in the cylinder."

The agent poked her fingers into the compartment, withdrew Dean's note and unfolded it. She read the note aloud so everyone could hear.

The supervisor looked at Dean and said, "Well, I guess that part of your story is true."

Everyone's attention was drawn to the door when there was a knock. The supervisor motioned for the potbellied man to open the door. As he opened the door, Dean saw his mother and said, "Mom!"

The supervisor said, "Tom, you, Sharon, and Cindy can go back to work. Please let that lady come in."

"I was waiting for you in the car, Dean. When you didn't come back from the terminal, I came to get you. Did you deliver your message?"

Dean nodded and said, "Yes, I tossed Roxy the airplane."

Cynthia stepped forward near the edge of the table and asked, "Why is my son in here? Is he in trouble?"

The supervisor shook her head and said, "We have to check everything that passes the detectors, that's all. The glider was unexpected, so we're investigating."

"So is Dean in trouble?"

"No, ma'am. But we want to warn him to avoid things like this from happening."

"What happened, Dean?"

"I didn't think I did anything wrong. I just wrote a note to Roxy and Dexie and put it in our glider, you know, the one we use to send messages to each other when we investigate things in Maxwells' backyard. I didn't think it would hurt anything, but the whole place went crazy like we were terrorists or something. That big guy grabbed me and brought me in here."

There was another knock on the door and the supervisor checked to see who it was, expecting a TSA agent, but instead seeing a woman with a concerned look on her face. The door was opened wider and Roxy saw her mother.

"Hi Mom! We're discussing the airplane and the note Dean tried to send us."

"So, is there something wrong, Roxy?

She shook her head. "I don't think so."

Roxy looked at the supervisor who had a scowl on her face, probably dealing with this particular situation for the first time.

"Well, I guess we should all get back to what we were doing before the glider entered restricted airspace," concluded the supervisor. She smiled, proud of her choice of words, and motioned for everyone to leave the room.

"Young man, do you want your airplane?"

Dean smiled and answered, "No ma'am. It has caused enough problems. You'd think I was trying to smuggle a sniper rifle in here."

Mary started toward the waiting area with Roxy. Dean and his mother went toward the exit door to the parking area. The plane was being held for Roxy and Mary; everyone else waiting had already boarded the jet.

"Ma'am!" shouted the supervisor, "You'll have to let me check your purse again since you left the secured area."

Roxy froze, thinking, "Oh no! She'll discover the Niffits! Our whole plan will be ruined and no one will be going to Japan!"

Roxy, her mom and the supervisor returned to the room where the woman in uniform said, "Please dump the contents of your purse on the table."

Mary hesitated, looked at Roxy, and slowly opened her purse. Mary didn't want to hurt the Niffits, so she tipped the purse sideways and everything slid out on the table.

Roxy put her hand over her mouth, afraid she would cry out, telling the supervisor to leave the little people alone, but the Niffits weren't in the purse. The supervisor reached down and scattered the items but found nothing abnormal and said, "Okay, you may board the plane. Have a nice trip."

Roxy and Mary tossed everything on the table back in the purse and they walked quickly to the boarding area. Roxy looked around to make sure no one would hear her and said, "Mom! Where are the Niffits?"

Chapter 18

Finding the Niffits

Dean and his mother had joined Mr. Maxwell and Dexie to explain what had happened in the room with the TSA people. Everything had taken place just as they had predicted, except for one thing, Roxy and Mary had been detained for some unknown reason.

Carl and Dexie boarded the plane and found their seats. Carl stood with Dexie watching passengers enter the plane from the jetway to find their seats, stow items in the overhead compartments, and sit down.

"There they are, Mr. Maxwell!" Dex pointed down the aisle toward the front of the plane.

Carl stood up so Roxy and Mary could see him.

Mary saw Carl, gave a little wave and fixed her eyes on her husband, seeing her seat location. Roxy and Mary didn't look very happy. As they moved slowly toward row 28, having to stop for people backing into the aisle, moving around and trying to get comfortable, Roxy couldn't stop asking herself where the Niffits had gone. Roxy sat down next to her dad and said, "Dad, we've lost the Niffits!"

Carl helped his wife get settled in the seat next to the window and looked back at Roxy.

"Tell me what happened, Rox."

Roxy told her dad what had happened when her mom's purse was dumped out on the table and how surprised they were when the Niffits weren't part of the contents of the purse.

Carl looked at Mary and said, "What do you think happened?"

"I've been racking my brain since we left that room and the only thing I can come up with is the Niffits must have climbed into another purse that looks like mine."

Mary leaned across in front of Carl and said, "Roxy, did you see anyone with a black purse similar to mine?"

Roxy looked up to the ceiling, closed her eyes, leaned her head all the way back against the seat and began forming a mental picture of the waiting area in the terminal. After about fifteen seconds, Roxy said, "Mom! There was a lady sitting two seats from you who had her purse on the floor to the left of her chair and your purse was on your right, so there was only one chair between the purses. I'll bet Akira and Masako climbed into that lady's purse! We have to find that lady!"

Mary said, "Oh! I remember her. She was wearing a light blue blazer, had glasses, and gray hair. The man sitting beside her had a light-yellow shirt and gray pants."

Dexie started to stand up saying, "Let's find that lady!"

She sat back down when one of the flight attendants said, "We will be in the air in about two minutes. Make sure everything is stowed and you have your seatbelts fastened."

Roxy grabbed Dex's arm, looked in her eyes, and said, "As soon as we're able to walk around, we'll track her down. Let's figure out what we're going to say."

In a few minutes, the captain made an announcement that they were at cruising altitude, but passengers should remain seated with seatbelts fastened in case of any turbulence.

Roxy looked at Dex, smiled and said, "I have to go to the bathroom!"

Dexie answered, "Me too! I'm about ready to pop!"

The girls released their seatbelts, moved into the aisle and moved in opposite directions, scanning the passengers as they slowly made their way down the corridor. Roxy spotted the lady, turned toward Dex, and motioned for Dex to join her. The girls were two rows behind the lady on her left. As they converged on the woman, they both pulled a niffit doll from their pockets.

"Excuse me, ma'am. Could you please look in your purse to see if there are any dolls like this in it?"

Dexie held up the doll representing Masako and Roxy showed the lady her Akira doll.

The lady put her magazine in her lap, gave the girls a frown and said, "I know there are no dolls like that in my purse, girls."

"How do you know without looking?" quizzed Roxy.

"Because I found them and gave them to a flight attendant. She said she had a place for lost and found items."

Dex replied, "Thank you, ma'am. Sorry we bothered you, but we would like to find our dolls."

The lady lifted up her magazine to resume reading and said, "That's all right. I hope you get them back."

Roxy and Dex looked at each other and said simultaneously, "Flight attendant!"

"Yes? What can I help you with, girls?"

A tall brunette with short hair, dressed in a dark-blue skirt and a white blouse was standing beside the girls.

Roxy was startled and said, "Oh, nothing."

Dex took over and said, "We've lost two of our dolls. This lady said she gave them to a flight attendant to put in the lost and found. Can you help us?"

Having recovered her senses, Roxy held up her niffit doll so the attendant, Coreen, could see what Dex was talking about.

"Oh, yes. I put them in the lost and found basket. I remember they were warm, seemed a little strange to me."

Roxy replied quickly, "They were in the back of the car in the sun and we put them in our pockets. We asked my mom to put them in her purse, but she put them in that lady's purse accidentally. Could we please get them?"

"Sure. Come with me, girls."

Dex looked at Roxy, raised her eyebrows and crossed her fingers as they followed Coreen to the galley area of the plane.

"Wait right here. I'll get them for you."

The girls watched the attendant open a cupboard and take out a wicker basket.

"Here they are."

Coreen picked up Akira and Masako in one hand and gave them to Roxy. Roxy stuck them in her shirt pocket and said, "Oh! Thank you, Coreen. You're a lifesaver!"

Coreen smiled and said, "You're welcome, girls. The dolls are still warm."

As the girls were returning to their seats, Dex said, "Actually she's a two lives saver," and the girls giggled.

Both girls glanced at the Niffits in Roxy's pocket and whispered, "Are you all right?" Akira and Masako both opened one eye and smiled. Masako gave a little wave.

Chapter 19

Returning Home

After the Maxwells, Dexie, and the Niffits landed in Japan, they found a hotel a few kilometers from the east coast and stayed overnight. The next day, they rode a commuter train to the coast and found a park where they said goodbye to the Niffits. Roxy and Dex carried the Niffits to a grassy area, gently placed them on the ground and whispered, "Goodbye and good luck." Akira and Masako bowed several times, waved good-bye, and disappeared into the tall grass.

Roxy and Dex both had tears in their eyes as they said goodbye to their little green friends. The girls were sad to bid them farewell but happy to have been able to help the Niffits return to their homeland.

"We did a good thing, Dex."

"I know, but I hate goodbyes, especially when it is to someone you love."

Roxy and Dex gave each other a hug and walked back to where Carl and Mary were waiting.

Mary said, "Are you girls all right?"

"Yes, Mom. We're just sad to see our friends go, but happy they are home. Masako will be in the best place to have her baby."

Carl said, "Well girls, how would you like to spend a few days in Hawaii?"

The girl's mood suddenly changed. Christmas time in Hawaii sounded exciting.

"When do we go?" Roxy inquired.

"I just made arrangements to go to the airport as soon as we get back to our hotel. Let's leave these big islands and go to some smaller ones. We'll stay a couple of days and fly back to Portland after we hit the beach and eat ourselves sick." Carl added, "I'm looking for a drink from a coconut shell."

The flight back to the mainland from Hawaii to Portland was uncomfortable for Roxy. She had gotten severely sunburned on the Waikiki beach and was miserable the last night in Hawaii, despite the lotion, cold drinks, and sleep.

Mary felt responsible and was keeping a watchful eye on her daughter. Roxy fell asleep as soon as they boarded the plane and Dex kept busy reading every magazine she could find on the airplane. She tried to watch a movie but couldn't concentrate on it. She finally had to talk with Mrs. Maxwell.

"Mrs. Maxwell?"

"Yes, Dexie?"

"I asked my mom, when she was a kid, what did she want to be when she grew up, but she just said she wanted to marry my father and be a housewife. Has Roxy talked to you about what she wants to study when she goes to college?"

"A little bit, Dexie. I told her not to worry about that, she has more than five years to think about it. Oh, she did mention she might like to be a pathologist or a sociologist. She loved working to get the Niffits back home."

About an hour from Portland, Roxy woke up and looked around the airplane. Her mom and dad were sleeping, like nearly everyone else, and Dexie was reading a book about travel destinations. Roxy thought, "I wonder what the Niffits are doing. Will we ever see them again?"

www.ingramcontent.com/pod-product-compliance
Lightning Source LLC
Chambersburg PA
CBHW042106160726
48295CB00017B/1000